A Professor Reflects
on Sherlock Holmes

Marino C. Alvarez

For my wife Victoria, a scholar herself, and to our son Christopher, a talented individual who continues to plot an intellectual path toward self-educating.

Contents

Foreword

He interrupted our meeting which in itself was not unusual, however, interrupting with a statement like this: "Excuse me, are you the Sherlock Holmes group? I have a paper I want to share?", is a bit different. This was the way Marino Alvarez wandered into the Nashville Scholars of the Three Pipe Problem, a scion society of the Baker Street Irregulars.

As Chief Investigator, I was intrigued by his boldness as he asked to read his paper to us. Our Scion is quite active, quite well known and quite scholarly so I just kept wondering to myself just who was the guy and why did he think he could come in and tell us some new about the master, Sherlock Holmes. As he began to read in his quiet unassuming voice, it was apparent why he was bold: this paper was excellent and worthy of the *Baker Street Journal*. My memory is that we all just sat there when he finished sort of star struck by this stranger who blew into our circle.

Soon, Dr. Alvarez was truly one of the Scholars. His sense of humor tempered with a quick wit made any absence apparent. When he and his wife could be with us, the meetings were brighter and "greener" since he had a keen interest in playing the game as all good Sherlockians do. But when he played, he played with a deep understanding of the Canon and an even deeper understanding of deduction. His academic background served him well as he helped unwind some of the mysteries as we worked for solutions to puzzling questions.

Personally, I have seen him literally take our small literary circle by storm as he and a few others truly uphold and proclaim the scholarship of our scion. Some of us simply like to sit back and passively play the game, but Dr. Alvarez plays each game with vigor and zeal. His study of the Canon and supporting material places him in rarified air with respect to scholars around the world. His writings on the writings prove clear to understand yet involved enough to keep your attention. As one of the Three Pipe Problems irregular Quizmasters, he always provides twists and turns coupled with the facts of the cases to make those gatherings festive to say the least.

As he travels the world for business and pleasure, Dr. Alvarez spreads the really good news about Sherlock Holmes and Dr. Watson. He is the Goodwill Scholar-Ambassador to the world and we live vicariously through him.

For those who are not familiar with his scholarship, a treat awaits them. His grasp of the Canon and his ability to tie the adventures to our world sets him apart. I hold his talent up to anyone without regret or fear. He is truly a Nashville Scholar of the Three Pipe Problem.

Billy Fields, Chief Investigator, Nashville Scholars of the Three Pipe Problem

Dr. Marino Alvarez is a true scholar, and a long-standing member of the Nashville Scholars of the Three Pipe Problem, established in 1979. He and his wife Dr. Victoria Risko Alvarez travel to international educators' meetings all over the world, invited as major presenters.

Usually quiet at meetings, you can be certain that his mind is busy, solving problems and coming up with solutions that others of us often miss. When he does comment we all listen attentively because we know there will be insight and knowledge coming from an engaged mind not unlike that of our literary hero, Sherlock Holmes.

Marino may even have a mind like Sherlock's smarter brother, Mycroft. But whatever wisdom comes from Marino is not dispensed as if it were the final answer, the super-thinker coming to save the rest of us in our muddling. No! He simply offers his solution or resolution of the perplexing mystery before us in a way that suggests he has given careful thought to the situation, has carefully arranged the pieces in his mind, and is offering a possible course correction, if you will. He is a deft facilitator in our discussions.

The world of Sherlock Holmes is all about ideas, possibilities, and lively discussions. It is a world all Sherlockians have chosen to participate in because we love the camaraderie of good friends and good debate. It seems possible that Arthur Conan Doyle wrote the stories just loosely enough for readers to find holes and dead ends and alternative paths that they could contemplate and arrive at a different conjecture before the problem is finally solved by Holmes himself.

This book engages the mind in the possibilities of that kind of thinking. It is dead center in the Sherlockian game of "what if…" "perhaps…" and "could it be…"; but Dr. Alvarez has also contributed background information and indisputable facts that bring more complete understanding to the canon, the sixty stories penned by Conan Doyle. Dr. Alvarez has provided a rich background of information about those holes, dead ends, and alternative paths. It is a reference to have at the ready, a literary mental warm-up to enjoy before, during, and after reading the canonical stories themselves.

In this book Dr Alvarez shares a rich treasure trove of thinking and experiences with us. I heartily recommend it as a blueprint for understanding the stories, for becoming familiar with the background of Conan Doyle's writing, and in preparation for full enjoyment of some of the best tales and mysteries ever written.

Jim Hawkins, Webmaster, Nashville Scholars of the Three Pipe Problem

Dr. Marino Alvarez has been a lover of the Sherlock Holmes stories since childhood and beyond. He enjoyed that fascination while getting his master's and doctoral degrees from the West Virginia University and became a noted and much published professor in the Department of Teaching and Learning of the College of Education and a senior researcher and Director of the Exploring Minds Project, in the Center of Excellence in Information Systems at Tennessee State University. Over the years he has employed his interest in Sherlock Holmes, especially the deductive methods of Holmes, to add sparkle to his books and lectures at scholarly educational conferences in many countries around the world. He has an active, playful sense of humor that helps him and his listeners and readers find the unexpected connections between the Victorian era of the Holmes stories and recent breakthroughs in education theory today. My main experience of Alvarez in action has been the delightful discussions and quizzes Marino leads on the Sherlockian novels and stories that we discuss at monthly meetings of the Nashville Scholars of the Three Pipe Problem and his major presentations at the Gathering of Southern Sherlockians in Chattanooga each year. He brings magic to his focus on Sherlock Holmes as consulting detective, scientist, and an academic who is insightful and curious in using his inquiring mind to seek answers as a fair-minded, critical, and imaginative thinker. When Alvarez gets a certain twinkle in his eyes, it signals us in his audience that a pun or humorous sidelight is on the way and will result in surprise and laughter. These essays reflect the same enjoyable spirit.

In assembling his book, Alvarez has used material from his Sherlockian presentations in many prestigious venues such from articles he has published in noteworthy publications such as the *Baker Street Journal*. Alvarez, to be sure, is scholarly, so some of these essays reflect the professor in him when he compares the writing styles of Holmes and Watson by counting the number of words per sentence and other such studies. My own favorite essays are his more colorful discussions of the Sherlockian stories and the travel accounts of him and his wife Vicki walking in the footsteps of Holmes and Watson in London and by traveling to the Reichenbach Falls at Meiringen, Switzerland, where Holmes was thought to have plunged to his death along with Professor Moriarty. They also make an impressive trip to the libraries of Oxford University to peruse the Sherlockian writings of Ronald Knox who in 1911, showed the world with a lecture at Oxford how the Sherlockian literary Game is played. Knox treated the stories as true to life and found ways to explain inconsistencies in a highly professional, literary way. Knox and Alvarez are brothers in the spirit of the game. In his book, Alvarez gives three examples of playing the Game with his own perky, wry, and incisive investigations of The Stockbroker's Clerk, The Engineer's Thumb, and The Valley of Fear. He does it well.

Gael Stahl, Chaplain/Historian, Nashville Scholars of the Three Pipe Problem

Acknowledgements

I thank the Nashville Scholars of the Three Pipe problem for their active involvement in our meetings, quizzes, and picnics. Their attendance at the monthly meetings and their scholarly interest in the Canon is constantly on display. Billy Fields is the Chief Investigator who directs our meetings. Gael Stahl, our chaplain and historian, with years of experience in our scion reveals the happenings. Kay Blocker is a charter member of the scion and along with Dean Richardson publishes our Newsletter, *Plugs and Dottles*. Bill Mason presents at Sherlockian meetings, has published his book of essays on Sherlock Holmes, and has contributed to the *Baker Street Journal*. David Hayes has made contributions to the Scholars Corner and is representative of the members of our group like Tom and Anita Feller who have developed quizzes for our monthly meetings. Jerome Boynton is always available to bring an artifact or two for our meetings that provides a genuine article related to a story under discussion. Jim Hawkins is our convener and the founder of Welcome Holmes and maintainer of the online discussion group (www.welcomeholmes.com). Jim is also our webmaster. He created and maintains our scion's website (nashvillescholars.net). His efforts are recognized for providing an international forum by which others may join in discussions about the stories. Other members are Rachel Lundberg, Nan Ottenbacher, Derek Martin, Carol Redding, Marj Stellar (charter member), Charlie Williams, Patsy King, Mary Margarette Jordan, Carol Garrett (charter member), Scott and Geeta McMillan, Michael and Cindy Parrish, Richard Keppler, Dee Raz, James Markham, Jeff Stewart, Stephanie Osborne, Robert McGrath, and Bill Markie. We have visits from our members in other states and countries such as, Carolyn and Joel Senter, Chris Redmond, Brad Keefauver, and Ronald Kritter. Lest we forget, we remember William C. Baker (charter member), David Bradley, Davice J. Sharpe, Vickie Smith (charter member), and Bob White.

The Beacon Society (www.beaconsociety.com/Index.htm) is also recognized as a group providing resources and recognition to teachers and students who keep alive the story elements of Arthur Conan Doyle's Sherlock Holmes. The Jan Stauber Grant is available for teachers and students who demonstrate and advocate the teaching and learning of the Canon. The website provides resources and examples for Sherlockians, teachers, students, and visitors. Among those members who are recognized are Marilynne McKay, webmaster, Francine Kitts, Joseph Coppola, Elaine Coppola, Carol Cavalluzzi, Susan Diamond, Andrew L. Solberg, P.J. Doyle, and Judith Freeman. My role has been to attend the yearly meetings and contribute a Sherlock Holmes Resume and a short adaptation of a play *The Red-Headed League*.

Several of these essays have been published in the *Baker Street Journal* and reprinted with the kind permission of Steven Rothman, editor, *The Baker Street Journal*. Others have been presented at the Gathering of Southern Sherlockians and at international and national literacy conferences. I thank Eric Conklin for permitting the reprint of his painting, Scott Bond for permission to use his illustration, and the photograph of the Union College football team in an 1887 scrapbook courtesy of Special Collections in the Schaffer Library at Union College, Schenectady, New York. Clare Hopkins, archivist, and Sharon Cure, librarian, Trinity College at Oxford were most gracious in granting permission and making available the papers of Monsignor Ronald A. Knox and the *Gryphon Book of Minutes*. I also thank Julian Reid, archivist, Merton College at Oxford for meeting with me and giving of his time through his communications. I compliment Roger Johnson, editor, of *The District Messenger*, the newsletter of the Sherlock Holmes Society of London for his timely updates and book reviews. His publication, like those of our own *Plugs and Dottles* and the many other Sherlockian scions throughout the world are valued resources that serve as records of the events that include writings, quizzes, informative interviews, book reviews, and reports of local happenings.

Prologue

Sherlock Holmes captured my interest as a young child while reading the short stories at bedtime. Within arm's reach was my volume of *The Complete Sherlock Holmes* published by Doubleday that served as my reading companion. Then the novels took on new meaning with additional characters, settings, and historical significance. As a former junior and high school teacher and then a college professor my interest in academic writings became assimilated with fictional portrayals

As a graduate student at West Virginia University I happened across a table of books that were on sale at the campus bookstore. One that captured my eye was, *A Doctor Enjoys Sherlock Holmes.* The author was Edward J. Van Liere, a physician and former Dean of the School of Medicine at West Virginia University. Over the years I have collected many books written on the life of Arthur Conan Doyle and those that depict and scrutinize Sherlock Holmes under various circumstances. However, my fingers gravitate to this one book by Van Liere that serves as the spark that ignites the telling of these essays from a perspective of a college professor.

My first Sherlock Holmes novel was acquired as an adolescent. Five of us teenagers were invited to a farm for the weekend. We each packed our gym bags and left the city for the country. On arrival in the early evening, we pitched our pup tents. Unintentionally, Danny stabbed the back of my left hand. This would not be the first incident with a knife. The next day, Saturday, we wandered through the fields and into an old barn. The barn was typical with bales of hay and scattered machinery, but it had stacks of books on wooden plank shelves. On the bottom was a book, *Conan Doyle's Best Books, volume 1*, with the novel A *Study in Scarlet* and other stories. It contains an introductory essay by Dr. Harold Emery Jones, "The Original Sherlock Holmes," who was a fellow-student with Conan Doyle. I began reading it and took the book to the tent. As the day progressed our food became scarce. Emotions were getting riled. By Sunday tensions started to rise. Pinky grabbed a couple of the few remaining hot dogs and holding a knife said, "These are mine." The knife wasn't the problem, it was the situation. It was the '50s; knives were commonplace in our neighborhood. I knew it was time to leave. Gary and Jerry agreed and we grabbed our gym bags, walked to the highway, and hitchhiked the twenty or so miles back to the city.

It is with this interest in Sherlockian minutiae that the essays within this book are told. The intent is to demonstrate that Sherlock Holmes has those traits necessary to be scholarly, and yet exhibit the qualities that exemplify the best in an effective professor.

He is insightful, curious, has an inquiring mind, seeks answers, is fair-minded, and is a critical and imaginative thinker.

This book is a collection of essays that have evolved from reading the fifty-six stories and four novels of the Sherlock Holmes adventures. Some of the essays draw on publications I wrote for *the Baker Street Journal* and *Reading Research and Instruction*, presentations made at Sherlockian gatherings and at international literacy conferences, and items appearing in a Case-Based Instruction video disc I developed of *The Red-Headed League*. The book focuses on Sherlock Holmes as a consulting detective, scientist, and academic. The essays in this volume reveal the writing styles of Dr. John Watson and Sherlock Holmes, Monsignor Knox's admonition to Dr. Watson, "You know my methods Watson: apply them!" and others that compare stories and the consistencies and inconsistencies that occur among them, "The Stock-Broker's Clerk: Parallels and Parodies," and "Thumbless in Eyford." One is a narrative of Sherlock Holmes' visit to Schenectady and American Football. Two essays focus on my journey to both Richenbach Falls and Trummelbach Falls and comparisons drawn between the two, and a visit to Trinity College in Oxford to view Monsignor Ronald A. Knox's papers and entries into the *Gryphon Book of Minutes*. References, Footnotes and Appendices are included within an essay so that continuity with the information can be readily associated. Several essays contain concept maps that I have developed to visually display the concepts and their relationships. Cmap Tools is the mapping tool that was used in constructing these visual arrangements.[1]

My approach is to relate what I knew about Sherlock Holmes and the period in which the stories took place. This took me beyond the structural elements of the story and into the historical, cultural, and societal milieu in which the stories were situated. It

---

[1] See IHMC Cmap Tools http://cmap.ihmc.us. Also, steps for developing concept maps are given in Marino C. Alvarez and D. Bob Gowin, *The Little Book: Conceptual Elements of Research* (Lanham, MD: Rowman & Littlefield, 2010),. 2-9; also D. Bob Gowin and Marino C. Alvarez, *The Art of Educating with V Diagrams* (New York and Cambridge UK: Cambridge University Press, 2005), 133-135.

is hoped that this book will be read by members of Sherlockian scions, serve as a resource for teachers and students, and will spark an interest to those readers interested in pursuing Sherlockian writings.

PART 1

ESSAYS

Simplifying Complexity in Sherlock Holmes Stores

"This complicates matters," said Gregson.
"Heaven knows, they were complicated enough
before." "You're sure it doesn't simplify them?"
Observed Holmes.

(*A Study in Scarlet*)

Each of us is the author of our own text. Whether the text is expository or narrative, in order for deliberate learning to occur we must first grasp the meaning intended by an author. Simplifying complexity demands that meaning must be a shared understanding between reader and author. This is accomplished by relating what we know about the content to new information provided in the prose. Our task is to find ways to make the unfamiliar more familiar. When reading a Sherlock Holmes story we want to use the clues to reach our own resolution and not wait for an explanation of his conclusions through Watson's writings. However this is a difficult task given the differing reasoning processes by Dr. Watson and the Inspectors at Scotland Yard when compared to those scientific and constructive abilities possessed by Sherlock Holmes.[2]

As we go through the events of a story, we are endlessly trying to simplify the complex by extracting net meanings. We use these clues to tie threads together. No matter how long the thread of meaning, it is important to be sure that the thread is not broken unless we are confronted with new information that prompts us to weave a new line of thought. We try to make sense of material presented to us by an author. For example, Sherlock Holmes sees the word "RACHE" and incurs a different meaning from that of Inspector Lestrade.[3] Clues are not always obvious so we need to rely on our on mental model of what constitutes a mystery story before, during, and when reaching a resolution of a story's outcome. A person's mental model is a representation of a particular belief based on existing knowledge of a physical system or a semantic representation depicted in a text. Our mental models are used to forecast events and to assess the accuracy of the events after they have been presented to us. As we learn about the instances of a story, we constantly test our interpretations of the world and, if necessary, revise our mental models as we experience and test alternative explanations throughout our readings. As we are confronted with characters, their predicaments, and the context of events that unfold during our reading it prompts us to become actively engaged with these structural elements, and facilitates theory building in anticipation of what lies ahead.

---

[2] See *2 + 2 ≠ 4?* in this volume.
[3] *A Study in Scarlet.*

Before reading a story, we know that there will be a beginning, middle, and a resolution when we finish. Also we are aware of the structural elements that comprise a text (e.g., theme, plot, setting, characters). However, a story may reveal more and add to our knowledge base if the reader goes beyond story elements. The Hundred Years War was a series of actions between England and France from 1337 to 1453. It was within this time period that the Siege of Harfleur took place in 1415. Henry the V landed in France and was victorious. This engagement at Harfleur was the setting for William Shakespeare to write:

> I see you stand like greyhounds in the slips,
> Straining upon the start. The game's afoot:
> Follow your spirit, and upon this charge
> Cry 'God for Harry, England, and Saint George!

> (*Henry V*, act III, scene 1)

This historical context and the play prompted Arthur Conan Doyle to use the phrase, "Come, Watson, come. The game is afoot" a well-known exclamation that some may attribute to a saying originating from Sherlock Holmes rather than from the pen of Shakespeare's *Henry V* in 1598.[4] However the exclamation does provide additional insight into this historical event and may prompt a reader to learn more about the era. To those interested in word etymology many of the words written by Shakespeare have different meanings today, but also have contributed to the mystery genre. Some words according to the *Oxford English Dictionary* include, arch-villain, bloodsucking, watchdog, assassination, bloodstained, catlike, go between, hint, reprieve, scuffle, shipwrecked, spectacled, upstairs, well-educated, well-behaved, well-bred, zany, among many others.

Monsignor Ronald A. Knox's essay, "Studies in the Literature of Sherlock Holmes," of 1911 raised the level of consciousness with a "higher criticism" in a humorous manner when reading the stories not only in finding inconsistencies within the stories but offering alternative interpretations as to what could be implanted to make the stories more credible. Dorothy L. Sayers became involved with this type of genre citing Ronald Knox, when she wrote about Sherlock Holmes.[5]

---

[4] *The Adventure of the Abbey Grange.*
[5] Dorothy L. Sayers, *Unpopular Opinions: Twenty-One Essays* (New York: Harcourt Brace, 1947), v-vi.

The rule of the game is that it must be played as solemnly as a county cricket match at Lord's; the slightest touch of extravagance or burlesque ruins the atmosphere.

When confronted with events that are factual they take us into a deeper level of consciousness; a place where curiosity arouses us to learn more about factual places, persons, and the circumstances surrounding these happenings. For example, in one of my writings, "The Valley of Fear: Three Missing Words," the story line prompted a deeper understanding of the mining conditions that existed in the Pennsylvania coal region and the connections among the events that occurred during this time period. A complete biography of Dr. Watson has been derived from piecing together the events depicted in the stories. His wartime service and medical studies at London University are just a few of these components.[6] The same has been done for Sherlock Holmes.[7]

Going beyond the text was a partial requirement when answering the questions to the Examination Paper, devised by R. Ivar Gunn.[8] The final question asks about factual events that require knowledge beyond the narrative in the text. "What do you know of the Duke of Balmoral?" "Matilda Briggs?"

Sherlock Holmes provides us with several precepts that need understanding when unraveling a story. Some of these I find important are:

- Given in six of the stories when speaking to Watson, "eliminate the impossible" and then analyze what remains as the source. (*The Sign of Four, The Adventure of the Beryl Cornet, The Adventure of the Blanched Soldier, The Adventure of the Bruce-Partington Plans, The Adventure of the Priory School, Silver Blaze*).

- Another is repeated in three other stories, "It is a capital mistake to theorize before one has data." (*A Scandal in Bohemia, The Adventure of the Second Stain, A Study in Scarlet*).

---

[6] See Desmond McCarthy, "Dr. Watson." In James Edward Holroyd, *Seventeen Steps to 221B* (London: George Allen & Unwin, 1967), 50-56.
[7] See Nick Rennison, *Sherlock Holmes: The Unauthorized Biography*, (London: Atlantic Books, 2005); also, Barry Day, *Sherlock Holmes: In His Own Words and in the Words of Those Who Knew Him*, (Lanham, MD: Taylor Trade Publishing, 2003).
[8] R. Ivar Gunn, "Examination Paper." In James Edward Holroyd, *Seventeen Steps to 221B*, (London: George Allen & Unwin, 1967), 179-182.

- A third precept, when reading the stories first look for an "alternative explanation "and then make reasoned judgments to either keep this as a working theory or to abandon it. (*The Adventure of Black Peter*).

- A fourth, cautions the reader against taking a "fact" as a mainstay. He states clearly, "There is nothing more deceptive than an obvious fact." (*The Boscombe Valley* Mystery).

- Perhaps a fifth of most importance, when reading a mystery is the use of "logic." Holmes' remarks, "Logic is rare. Therefore it is upon the logic rather than upon the crime that you should dwell." (*The Adventure of the Copper Beeches*).

- A sixth is to trace the events and look for "consistency." Holmes states, "We must look for consistency. Where there is want of it we must suspect deception." (*The Problem of Thor Bridge*).

- Finally, we should not neglect "backward reasoning." This is an important concept that Holmes uses when solving his cases. "There are fifty who can reason synthetically for one who can reason analytically." (*A Study in Scarlet*).

Despite our awareness of these and other precepts that may come to mind, many of the stories once explained still need a Watson exclamation, "How absurdly simple!"[9] Watson is a testament to philosopher Alfred North Whitehead's statement, "Simplicity this side of complexity is simplistic, worth nothing; but simplicity the other side of complexity is worth everything."[10] The message to both readers and authors serves as a caution. When confronted with complexities of understanding, learn from what is written and read so that in the process what is learned can change the meaning of experience and lead to new meanings.

Mindful Inquiry

Simplifying complexity also takes into consideration mindful inquiry: the ability to view situations or problems from multiple perspectives rather than following one linear path of inquiry to achieve a specified outcome. Simplifying complexity demands thoughtful resolution through mindful inquiry which may or may not result in finality.

---

[9] The Adventure of the Dancing Men.
[10] Alfred North Whitehead, In W.H. Auden and L. Kronenberger (Eds.). *The Viking Book of Aphorisms* (New York: Penguin Books, 1966).

Some traits exhibited by Sherlock Holmes when using reasoned inquiry to make sense of an educative event are:

1. Makes judgments based on facts. (*A Study in Scarlet, The Sign of Four, The Hound of the Baskervilles, The Valley of Fear, A Scandal in Bohemia*).

2. Views reality from several possible perspectives eliminating those based on inference (*The Sign of Four, The Boscombe Valley Mystery, The Adventure of Silver Blaze, The Adventure of the Dancing Men*).

3. Grasps meaning of the event and uses it as a process to reach a given outcome (*A Study in Scarlet, The Hound of the Baskervilles, The Adventure of the Speckled Band, The Adventure of the Copper Beeches, The Adventure of the Gloria Scott, The Adventure of the Dancing Men, The Five Orange Pips*).

4. Uses personal experience to govern his approach to problem solving (*A Study in Scarlet, The Hound of the Baskervilles, The Valley of Fear, The Adventure of the Reigate Squire, The Adventure of Black Peter, The Adventure of the Six Napoleons, The Adventure of the Bruce-Partington Plans, The Adventure of the Three Gables*

5. Is able to abandon personal beliefs and shift his perspectives during a case investigation (*The Man With The Twisted Lip, The Adventure of the Blue Carbuncle, The Adventure of the Copper Beeches, The Adventure of the Creeping Man, The Problem of Thor Bridge*).

6. Uses knowledge and skills that are appropriate to a given set of circumstances and weighs their effectiveness during the course of the investigation (*A Study in Scarlet, The Sign of Four, The Hound of the Baskervilles, The Valley of Fear. The Red-Headed League, The Boscombe Valley Mystery*

7. Relies on a variety of books to guide his inquiry (*The Valley of Fear, A Scandal in Bohemia, The Adventure of the Noble Bachelor, The Adventure of the Musgrave Ritual, The Adventure of the Empty House, The Adventure of the Six Napoleons, The Adventure of the Three Students, The Adventure of the Lion's Mane*).

8. Uses his imagination to solve novel problems (*A Study in Scarlet, The Hound of the Baskervilles, The Valley of Fear, The Boscombe Valley Mystery, The Adventure of Silver Blaze, The Adventure of the Norwood Builder, The Adventure of Black Peter, The Adventure*

of the Devil's Foot, The Problem of Thor Bridge, The Adventure of the Lion's Mane, The Adventure of the Retired Colourman).

Simplifying complexity lies in being able to comprehend complex ideas and resolving them by either engaging in critical and problem-solving introspectively, or perhaps sharing meaning with others so as to go to the "other side of complexity" to make these complex ideas or situations meaningful. Comprehension also includes an understanding of the author's style of organizing information, point of view, choice of words, and particular language structures. These considerations may enable us to better grasp the intentions of an author, such as A. Conan Doyle, and enable us to delve more into the historical, societal, cultural, and political aspects in which a story takes place.

Sherlock Holmes and Educating

*Desultory readers are seldom remarkable for
the exactness of their learning.*

(A Study in Scarlet)

When reading the stories in the Canon the images of the historical, societal, and cultural milieu of Victorian England in 1895 are always present. If we look at a resume of Sherlock Holmes we are able to discern the many qualities he embraces and enables us to better understand the context in which he is portrayed in the stories (see Figure 1).

Figure 1. Sherlock Holmes Resume.

SHERLOCK HOLMES
Consulting Detective

221B Baker Street
St. Marylebone
London, England

EDUCATION
1872-1876 Attended an English university, although neither dates nor location is certain. Arguments are made for both Oxford (Christ Church College) and Cambridge (perhaps Sidney Sussex or Caius College)

PERSONAL
Born January 6, 1854 (W.S. Baring-Gould. *Sherlock Holmes of Baker Street*. New York: Bramhall House, 1962)
Son of Siger Holmes and Violet Sherrinford Holmes (Baring-Gould, *above*)
Brother Mycroft Holmes resides in Pall Mall opposite the Diogenes Club, Whitehall District, London, England. "He *is* the British Government." (BRUC)*
Grandson of a sister of the French artist Émile Jean-Horace Vernet (GREE)
Rented rooms in Montague Street, London, England (MUSG)
Main residence at 221B Baker Street, London, England (STUD)
Retirement in South Downs, Sussex, England (LAST)

For a list of the 4-letter abbreviations for Canonical stories see www.nashvillescholars.net/scholarstoryabbrevs.htm

EXPERIENCE
1880 Formally declared a professional career as the first consulting detective (GLOR)

1881 Meets and shares an apartment with Dr. John H. Watson at 221B Baker Street. Dr. Watson shares in many investigations and chronicles many Sherlock Holmes adventures (STUD)
1881-1903 Professional practice
1891-1894 Hiatus (EMPT)
1903 or 1904 Retired; beekeeper in Sussex Downs (LION) (see Vincent Starrett, *The Private Life of Sherlock Holmes*. Chicago, IL: University of Chicago Press, 1960, p. 35;also, Baring-Gould, above, Appendix I)
1904-Present [Little-known fact] Professor (M.C. Alvarez. "Sherlock Holmes As College Professor," *Baker Street Journal*. 51, no. 1, 2001, 44-48,
1907 Involved with a case (LION)
1914 Involved with a case (LAST)

PUBLICATIONS
Books
1. The Book of Life (STUD)
2. Practical Handbook of Bee Culture, with Some Observations upon the Segregation of the Queen (LAST)
3. The *Whole Art of Detection*, a textbook in preparation (ABBE)

Monographs
4. *On Secret Writings* (DANC)
5. *Upon the Distinction between the Ashes of the Various Tobaccos* (STUD, SIGN, BOSC)
6. *On the Typewriter and Its Relation to Crime* (IDEN)
7. *Upon the Tracing of Footsteps* (SIGN)
8. *Upon the Influence of a Trade upon the Form of the Hand* (SIGN)
9. *Of Tattoo Marks* (REDH)
10. *Upon the Dating of Old Documents* (HOUN, GOLD)
11. *On the Polyphonic Motets of Lassus.* Printed for private circulation (BRUC)
12. *Chaldean Roots in the Ancient Cornish Language* (DEVI)
13. *On the Surface Anatomy of the Human Ear.* Two articles in the Anthropological Journal (CARD)
14. *Malingering* (DYIN)
15. *Early English Charters,* in progress (3STU)
16. *Upon the Uses of Dogs in the Work of the Detective,* in progress (CREE)

KNOWLEDGE AND CHARACTERISTICS
Six feet tall, dark hair, lean build
Knowledge of chemistry – profound (STUD)
Literate – enjoys a collection of a variety of books
Master of disguises: a bookseller (EMPT), a groom (SCAN), a clergyman (SCAN), an opium addict (TWIS), an old Italian priest (FINA), a seaman (SIGN), a plumber (CHAS), an old woman (MAZA)
Literary knowledge and language proficiency in French and Latin (Harry Shefter (Ed). *Reader's Supplement for the Great Adventures of Sherlock Holmes*, New York: Washington Square Press, 1972)
Well-versed in philosophy

Expert knowledge of beekeeping (LAST)
Expert in noticing and observing:
  - able to discern characteristics of physical objects such as a pocket watch (SIGN) or a walking
    stick (HOUN), as well as animal characteristics such as tracks (e.g., cows, horses), and their
    features.
  - developed a functional test for blood stains (STUD)
    can identify characteristics revealed by typewritten documents (IDEN)
  - distinguishes different types of shoe prints, footprints, horseshoe prints, and hound dog
    prints.
  - able to identify different types of bicycle tires and their impressions, track prints revealed by
    the of carriages.
   - knowledgeable in the types of tobacco ashes and can identify the kinds of cigarettes found at
    a crime scene
Plays the violin (STUD)
Musical scholar. (see Oliver Mundy, *Sherlock Holmes and Music*. Cited in Camden House,
www.ignisart.com/camdenhouse/scholars/SHOLMES_AND_MUSIC.pdf
Enjoys attending concerts (REDH)
Browses in art galleries (HOUN)

ATHLETIC SKILLS
Boxer (GLOR, YELL)
Fencer (GLOR)
Baritsu (or Bartitsu), a martial art of Japanese wrestling (EMPT)
Martial art of singlestick: a weapon made of wood, taking the form of a cane (STUD)
Knowledge of golf clubs (GREE)
Marksman with pistol (MUSG)

REFERENCES
John H. Watson, M.D. 221B Baker Street, London, England. Or c/o Dr. Watson, Paddington
district
Inspector Lestrade of Scotland Yard, London, England
Inspector Tobias Gregson of Scotland Yard, London, England
Inspector Stanley Hopkins of Scotland Yard, London, England
Inspector MacDonald of Scotland Yard, London, England
Mrs. Martha Hudson, landlady, cook, and housekeeper, 221A Baker Street, London, England
(*Aside*: Inquiries for Mrs. Hudson should be confined to my professional activities; tenant queries
should be avoided).

POSTSCRIPT It is always 1895

Sherlock Holmes' resume provides an overview of the talents and qualities he possesses. He is the first consulting detective; knowledgeable in an array of literary, scientific, philosophical ideologies, languages, the arts; and displays athletic proficiency in boxing, single stick, fencing, and Baritsu. This resume serves as a blueprint for mapping his accomplishments and knowledge areas providing background information we can draw on when reading his stories. It may provide a framework couched in the year 1895 that takes us to that period where we hear the horses' hoofs of the hansom cab, the sounds of the steam engine and the tracks beneath our railway carriage; a time period when rain and fog are the backdrop providing the setting for the yet unknown to be revealed.

This resume provides a "mind set" as we begin to read a story. For example, I ask myself questions about the historical period:

- When was the time period of stories?
- What's happening in London?
- Who's the Queen during this period? How did she influence the history, culture, and people of this time period?
- What kinds of transportation were used during this historical period in London and the surrounding countryside?
- Who were the writers, scientists, artists, mathematicians, musicians, historians of this period?

When reading a story I can better understand the circumstances in which the setting, theme, plot, and characters are evolving by keeping in mind the social and working conditions of the era:

- How does the economic and social setting of the story relate to present-day surroundings in Great Britain, the United States; another country?
- What were the working conditions for teenagers during this time in history?
  - Did the conditions faced by the Baker Street Irregulars make them less conspicuous and more observant?
- Who were the mystery writers of this time period? Scientists? Play writers? Historians? Musical Composers? Artists?
  - Why were they important?

21B Baker Street

In a similar vein it is helpful to have an image of the residence of 221B Baker Street if we are to imagine the events that transpire within these walls (see Figure 2). This drawing is taken from the *Strand Magazine* showing what the Sherlock Holmes Flat might have resembled.[11]

Figure 2. Sherlock Holmes' Rooms.

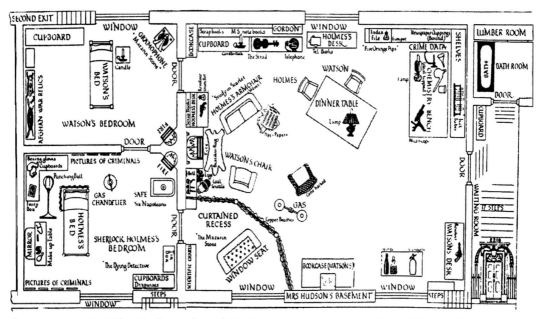

Source: Ernest H. Short's floor plan of 221B Room, circa 1948, and published in the *Strand* magazine in 1950. Retrieved from Chris Redmond's. http://www.sherlockian.net. October 12, 2011.

We are privy to the visitors who come to tell their stories and aided by the visual image of where these discussions are taking place. We have a notion of what is meant when clients are asked to sit in a particular chair, or when a reference is made to the tobacco in the slipper, or the chemical table in the corner, or when observations are made from the bow window about a passerby. For example, we have a setting when Holmes writes:

---

[11] Paul McPharlin, with the aid of an architect, R. Spearman Myers, has painstakingly, reconstructed the dwellings of 221B Baker Street using the stories as a guide, and describes how it would have been furnished and constructed in the historical period of the time. See "221B Baker Street: Certain Physical Details," *Baker Street Journal*, vol. 2. no. 2, 1947, 180-194.

It is my habit to sit with my back to the window and to place
my visitors in the opposite chair, where the light falls full upon
them.

(*The Adventure of the Blanched Soldier*)

The sketch provides a referent to these descriptions when reading a story and provides a context to actively engage in the story's events.

As we read the stories it is also enabling to know about the literary agent, A. Conan Doyle, and the two principals, Sherlock Holmes and Dr. James H. Watson. The stories reveal characters associated with Sherlock Holmes such as his brother Mycroft and Mrs. Hudson from whom both he and Watson lease their flat. Wayne and Francine Swift cogently acquaint the reader with those associates with whom Sherlock Holmes encounters in his stories.[12] In their article they categorize the circumstances when Homes was consulted, crimes that were committed during the case, his clients and victims, the members of the police, and his adversaries.

Educating

When we are confronted with new or unfamiliar information this material must become integrated with the old, familiar ideas and meanings we already know. Reading a Sherlock Holmes story brings us into the happenings of the time period. This requires a more thorough understanding of the culture, social, and political milieu to which the events take place. Bridging the gap from the present to the past influences how new learning occurs. During our reading we construct ideas about how the world of Sherlock Holmes works. For educating to occur, both the affective, connotative, and cognitive domains work together to achieve meaning through the interaction of thinking, feeling, and acting.

Every field has its claims for criteria of excellence. The criteria of excellence used in the study of literary works of art fall into groups around four elements: the work of art itself, the artist making the work, the audience experiencing the work, and the universe about which the work evolves.[13] A work may be judged for its internal coherence, the artist judged for imagination, expressivity, and craftsmanship; the audience may judge

---

[12] Wayne and Francine Swift, "The Associates of Sherlock Holmes. *Baker Street Journal*, vol. 49, no. 1, (March, 1999): 25-45.

[13] Max H. Abrams, *The Mirror and the Lamp: Romantic Theory and the Critical Tradition* (Oxford University Press, New York, 1953).

the work by standards of edification and entertainment, and the universe pertains to realism, accuracy, and truthfulness. Different theories of literary criticism balance these four sources of criteria of excellence in different ways. These criteria have been applied to the writings of Sherlockian stories and have undergone critical analyses. The popularity of Sherlock Holmes and the stories still continue to be read, extended by pastiches, portrayed in art, and shown in films.

Significant learning is the reconstruction of human experience as that experience changes from a strong feeling of involvement to a strong knowledge yielding power and mastery. In these essays, concept maps are used to convey the meaning of ideas. They are flexible, and concept rankings can be shifted to show new organizations of ideas. The stories provide fertile ground for new meaning to occur. This new meaning is dependent upon what we already know about the literary setting and societal and political environment of the period. Our present knowledge gives us the power for new knowledge to be acquired. For us as learners, two things are of utmost importance: what we claim to know; and what we need to know. Delving into a story's context, beyond its structural elements, gives us greater opportunities to enlighten our conceptual understanding of the time, place, and cultural significance that a story affords.

The art of educating is something we do for ourselves.[14] No one can do it for us. Grasping a meaning not our own and then using that grasped meaning for learning is an event of deep understanding. We learn about managing our own learning. We experience situations that demand the asking of questions first and constructing answers to our questions. In our reading we anticipate possibilities, sift through the facts and clues, and make speculations for plausible resolutions. Learning for oneself reduces complexities – simplifying the notion of learning through creative, imaginative, caring, reasoning, and critical thinking and understanding is the primary aim of educating.

---

[14] Marino C. Alvarez and D. Bob Gowin, *The Little Book: Conceptual Elements of Research.* (Lanham, MD: Rowman & Littlefield, 2010); also, D. Bob Gowin and Marino C. Alvarez, *The Art of Educating with V Diagrams* (New York and Cambridge UK: Cambridge University Press, 2005).

Dr. Watson vs. Sherlock Holmes's Writing Style

*"Why do you not write them yourself?" I said,
with some bitterness." I will, my dear Watson,*

(*The Adventure of the Abbey Grange*)

Sherlock Holmes has generated much current interest due to the recent releases of the Sherlock Holmes films, and the publishing of graphic novels and pastiches. These films and new publications take Sherlock beyond the pages of the fifty-six stories and four novels written by Dr. John H. Watson and published by his literary agent A. Conan Doyle. But the original stories and novels need to be read and reread to understand the situated contexts in which the characters, places, and events within the stories are centered. The varied neighborhoods whether in a city, rural community, or foreign land provide the reader with landscapes that not only "set" the scene but also reveal opportunities for discoveries that go beyond the plot.

Charles Press has noted that while Victorian prose is used in the writing of the stories, the style of writing does little to impede the readings and even embellishes their appeal.[15] Yet when reading these stories there is a variety of factors that affect readability. One is the use of specialized vocabulary requiring the reader to understand sentences within the circumstances in which the word appears. For example, in the "The Red-Headed League," Dr. Watson describes Jabez Wilson's appearance as, "He wore rather baggy gray shepherd's check trousers, a not overclean black frock-coat, unbuttoned in the front, and a drab waistcoat with a heavy, brassy Albert chain, and a square pierced bit of metal dangling down as an ornament." Such words within this one sentence needing clarification may be: "baggy," "shepherd's check trousers," "frock-coat," "waistcoat," and "a brassy Albert chain." The "Albert chain," is a heavy metal watch chain named for Prince Albert, the husband of Queen Victoria. This definition of an "Albert chain" may arouse our curiosity and take us to a deeper understanding of the historical period during the reign of Queen Victoria and to perhaps learn how the "Albert chain" came about in one's wardrobe. A writing style not only informs but can initiate a curiosity that enables us to better understand the culture and dress of a story's setting. In this same story, is a Latin phrase *Omne ignotum pro magnifico* translated to read, "Whatever is not understood seems greater than it really is." Or a word that may not be part of our vocabulary such as "derbies" once defined as "handcuffs," becomes

---

[15]Charles Press, *Looking Over Sir Arthur's Shoulder*, "Readability: Overcoming the Perils of Victoria Prose" (Shelburne, Ontario: George A. Vanerburgh, Publisher, 2004), 32.

meaningful and extends our knowledge. Words and their meaning are crucial for a reader's understanding of the events that are taking place within a story.

In addition to words that may not be known or have multiple meanings, or foreign phrases that need explanation, are many other factors that need to be considered when pairing a reader with a Sherlock Holmes story, in particular, and other narrative and expository texts in general. The purpose of this essay is to examine three stories, written by Dr. Watson, about three professors. I chose these three stories since the professors share with me similar academic and university backgrounds. I then compare these three to two stories written by Sherlock Holmes using the Fry Readability Formula.

Dr. Watson's Writing Style

Much has been written about Dr. Watson's writings of the stories contained within the Canon. Some have criticized his recollection of events, arguing that there may be discrepancies in the telling of the events that took place, or incorrect recordings of the dates. However, little has been written about his writing style or his level of appeal to readability. Of course, readability is more than the ease or difficulty of a text determined by a formula. Such formulas do not take into consideration an individual's motivational interest, background knowledge and experiences brought to the text materials that often override difficult vocabulary or writing style.

Professor Charles E. Lauterbach approached difficulty by counting the words in each of the fifty-six short stories and four novels contained in *The Complete Sherlock Holmes* (New York: Garden City Publishing Company, 1938).[16] He used an electronic counter and calculated a reliability measure with "The Adventure of the Veiled Lodger" that yielded 4,499 words in the first count and 4.498 in the second. He concluded that his count was within a one-word difference, and thus a reliable representation of number of words in the story. I used the same story appearing in Camden House to compare Professor Lauterbach's findings against those obtained by using the Microsoft Document word count option.[17] The results showed a word count of 4,497. This number is consistent with that obtained by Professor Lauterbach.

---

[16] Charles E. Lauterbach, "The Word Length of the Adventures of Sherlock Holmes," *Baker Street Journal*, vol. 10, no. 2 (April, 1960): 101-104.
[17] Camden House . *The Complete Sherlock Holmes*, http://www.ignisart.com/camdenhouse/. Retrieved October 12, 2011.

Table 1 compares the word count obtained using the Microsoft Document word option of three stories I am focusing on in this essay.[18] These three stories are similar in the number of words obtained by Professor Lauterbach.

Table 1. Word Count Comparisons of Three Stories.

	Word Count	
Story	Microsoft Word Count	Professor Lauterbach
The Final Problem	7.191	7,203
The Creeping Man	7,710	7,726
The Golden Pince-Nez	8,970	8,989

Knowing the number of words in a given story, while interesting, does little to reveal either the writing style or difficulty of a story. However, a 100 word count combined with the length of sentences within these 100 words can determine an "estimate" of ease or passage difficulty of a story. A readability formula gives the user an approximate "estimate" of passage difficulty and a grade level. I stress the word "estimate" in that these kinds of formulas cannot provide an absolute reading level of a text. Also such formulas are often misused in educational settings by applying them to reading materials and held to represent an arbitrary and exact reading level. Readability formulas are but one measure of a text's reading ease or difficulty. The readability level derived from these formulas measure sentence length as a constant with either word length or percent of unfamiliar words depending on the formula used to assess text difficulty. Among the variables *not* measured by readability formulas include: grammar, syntax, use of slang, concept word level, reader background, reader interest, size of print, words with multiple meanings, and obscure or archaic words. [19]

---

[18] *The Final Problem, The Adventure of the Creeping Man,* and *The Adventure of the Golden Pince-Nez.*

[19] Others have used the Flesch Readability Formula to assess Sherlock Holmes stories with type of words and readability measures. See Pasquale Accardo, *Diagnosis and Detection, The Medical Iconography of Sherlock Holmes,* (London: Associated University Press, 1987); Charles Press, *Looking Over Sir Arthur's Shoulder,* "Readability: Overcoming the Perils of Victoria Prose," (Shelburne, Ontario: George A. Vanerburgh, Publisher, 2004); Wayne and Francine Swift, "The Associates of Sherlock Holmes," *Baker Street Journal,* vol.49, no. 1 (March, 1999). The Flesch measures sentence length and word length like the Fry Readability formula, but counts sentences differently in that a sentence that has periods, explanation points, colons and semicolons serve as sentence delimiters

In accordance with the Fry Readability Formula guidelines, I implemented the following procedures.[20] First, I selected randomly a 100-word passage from each of the specified five stories. Second, I counted the number of sentences within these hundred words estimating the last sentence to the nearest tenth. Third, I counted and recorded the number of syllables of this one hundred word passage. Fourth, the total number of sentences and total number of syllables per sentences for each passage was divided by 3.

The results were applied to the Fry Graph to determine the approximate instructional reading level of the story. This procedure was repeated with the other two stories written by Dr. Watson. Story by passage and number of sentences and syllables per 100 words are shown in Table 2.

Table.2. Story by passage and number of sentences and syllables per 100 words.

Story	Passage	No. of Sentences Per 100 Words	No. of Syllables Per 100 Words
The Final Problem	1	2.4	147
	2	4.9	135
	3	5.5	135
Total		12.8	417
		12.8 ÷ 3 = 4.26	417 ÷ 3 = 139
The Creeping Man	1	5.0	136
	2	3.9	134
	3	3.4	134
Total		12.3 ÷ 3 = 4.1	404 ÷ 3 = 135
The Golden Pince-Nez	1	3.8	142
	2	5.6	134
	3	6.3	114
Total		15.7 ÷ 3 = 5.23	390 ÷ 3 = 130

The comparisons of the approximate instructional grade level of each of the stories are given in Table 3.

---

and denotes the end of a sentence. The range of application for the Fry is 1 – college; Flesch, 5 – college. Both the Fry and the Flesch have a standard error of estimate in terms of grade level as approximately 1.00.

[20] Edward Fry, "Fry's Readability Graph: Clarifications, Validity, and Extension to Level 17." *Journal of Reading*, Vol. 21, No. 3 (December, 1977): 242-252.

Table 3. Approximate Instructional Reading Level of the Three Stories.

Story	Total No. of Sentences Per 100 words ÷ 3	Total No. of Syllables Per 100 words ÷ 3	Approximate Instructional Grade Level
The Final Problem	4.26	139	9
The Creeping Man	4.10	135	9
The Golden Pince-Nez	5.23	130	7

Interestingly, two stories fall within the 9th grade reading level; the other story approximately two levels lower. Of equal importance is the total number of words and syllables when comparing the three stories. The total number of sentences given in both *The Final Problem* and *The Creeping Man* are within the 4.0 range; while *The Golden Pince-Nez* registers slightly above 5.0. However, when examining the total number of syllables across the three stories they are somewhat similar. This example illustrates that a readability formula can be manipulated to yield a reading "ease" or "difficulty" of a text depending on the number of sentences and word length within a one hundred word passage. When comparing these three stories, the higher number of sentences in the selected passages from *The Golden Pince-Nez* influenced the results of a lower reading level.

Sherlock Holmes' Writing Style

Dr. Watson challenges Sherlock Holmes to write his own narratives:

"I must admit, Watson, that you have some power of selection, which atones for much which I deplore in your narratives. Your fatal habit of looking at everything from the point of view of a story instead of as a scientific exercise has ruined what might have been an instructive and even classical series of demonstrations. You slur over work of the utmost finesse and delicacy, in order to dwell upon sensational details which may excite, but cannot possibly instruct, the reader."

"Why do you not write them yourself?" I said, with some bitterness.
"I will, my dear Watson,
(*The Adventure of the Abbey Grange*)

In *The Case-Book of Sherlock Holmes,* Sherlock Holmes writes two of his own exploits in the first person: "The Adventure of the Blanched Soldier" and "The Adventure of the Lion's Mane." I randomly selected three passages from each of these two stories and applied the Fry Readability Formula to determine if there was a difference in the number of sentences and syllables, and degree of ease or reading difficulty when compared to Dr. Watson's three stories. The procedures were identical to the ones given above for Dr. Watson's three stores. Table 4 reports the findings when comparing the number of sentences and syllables for the "The Adventure of the Blanched Soldier" and "The Adventure of the Lion's Mane."

To avoid undue confusion with the numbers appearing in Table 4 under "The Lions Mane," I selected three random passages from the story, "The Adventure of the Lion's Mane." All three 100 word passages are shown in the table. A problem arose with passage 2 in that the number of sentences far exceeded those in passages one and three. However, the number of syllables for these three passages is relatively within range of acceptability. When the three passages were averaged by total number of sentences and syllables the application to the Fry Graph yielded a reading level of 6. This finding seemed to be incongruent given the range of sentence discrepancy. Directions for the Fry Graph suggest adding another passage when there is such an inconsistency. These results with the substitute passage 2 are included within Table 4.

Table 4. Story by passage and number of sentences and syllables per 100 words.

Story	Passage	No. of Sentences Per 100 Words	No. of Syllables Per 100 Words
The Blanched Soldier	1	7.2	123
	2	2.9	131
	3	4.2	154
Total		12.8	417
		14.3 ÷ 3 = 4.76	408 ÷ 3 = 136
The Lion's Mane	1	4.9	132
	2	*10.0	132
	3	4.6	126
Total		19.5 ÷ 3 = 6.5	390 ÷ 3 = 130
**Substitute Passage 2		5.7	134
		25.1 ÷ 4 = 6.2	524 ÷ 4 = 131
***Removal Passage 2		5.7	134
		15.2 ÷ 3 = 5.0	392 ÷ 3 = 130

*Note the discrepancy in the number of sentences when compared to the other two passages.
**Substitute passage 2 replacement yields 5.7; 134. When combining the four passages and dividing by 4, the averge of total number of syllables equals 6.2 and the total number of sentences equal 131.
***When passage 2 is removed as the outlier, the substitute passage averaged with passages one and two yield 5.7 and 134.

The comparisons of the approximate instructional grade level of the two stories are given in Table 5.

Table 5. Approximate Instructional Reading Level of the Two Stories.

Story	Total No. of Sentences Per 100 words ÷ 3	Total No. of Syllables Per 100 words ÷ 3	Approximate Instructional Grade Level
The Blanched Soldier	4.76	136	8
The Lion's Mane	6.50	130	6
*Four Passages (÷ 4)	6.20	131	7
**Substitute Passage	5.70	392	7

Searching the Clues for Misinterpretations

The two stories vary when the total number of sentences and syllables are each divided by 3 and applied to the Fry Graph. When we look at the second passage that was first randomly selected for "The Adventure of the Lion's Mane," the number of short sentences within this selection is 10.0. The second substitute passage has a sentence count of 5.7. However, in both of these passages the syllable count is the same, 134.

A further examination of passage 2 from "The Adventure of the Lion's Mane" that was selected initially provides clues about the lower reading level assigned to this story. In passage 2, ten sentences appeared and this number of sentences is greatly different from the number of sentences assigned to passages 1 and 3 (4.9 and 4.6, respectively). Passage 2 is shown below:

Passage 2

"At the very place." The words stood out clear in my memory. Some dim perception that the matter was vital rose in my mind. That the dog should die was after the beautiful, faithful nature of dogs. But "in the very place." Why should this lonely beach be fatal to it?

Was it possible that it also had been sacrificed to some revengeful feud? Was it possible? Yes, the perception was dim, but already something was building up in my mind. In a few minutes I was on my way to The Gables, where I found Stackhurst in his study. "

A substitute passage – chosen randomly from the same story – was selected to verify the reported reading level.[21] This substitute passage contained 5.7 sentences and when combined with passages 1 and 3 yielded a reading level that seems consistent with the reading levels of the remaining stories (grades 8 and 7, respectively).

Readability Checklists provide the user of readability formulas with more insight. A more comprehensive text review would be to use a Readability Checklist such as the one presented in Vacca, Vacca, and Mraz that provides a more comprehensive assessment of a text rather than relying on a number alone.[22] In this checklist three areas of focus are understandability, usability, and interestability. The first area contains

---

[21] The directions for the Fry Readability Graph state, "If a great deal of variability is found in syllable count or sentence count, putting more samples into the average is desirable."
[22] Richard T. Vacca, Jo Anne Vacca and Maryann Mraz, *Content Area Reading* (Boston: Pearson, 2011), 113-119.

statements intended to assess the relationship between the reader's prior knowledge with the text's material. For example, are the assumptions about students' vocabulary knowledge appropriate? A second area, usability, contains two subsections: external and internal organizational features. External organizational features include whether the table of contents provides a clear overview of the text's content; the clarity of major and subheadings; and the degree to which visual aids are enablers to understand concepts. Internal evaluations include the inclusion of clear statements that define technical vocabulary; and whether the author uses patterns of organization to assist students in interpreting the text. The purpose of these statements is to determine characteristics of a writing style that can affect comprehension. The third domain of inquiry is interestability which is designed to assess the writing style and motivational purpose of a text and its accompanying materials.

Using a readability formula in concert with a readability checklist can provide more insight into a given text. Teachers use these assessments as guides rather than absolute measures to match reading materials to their students' interests and abilities. In the case of Dr. Watson the assessment as to his writing style and approximate level of reading ability with the random samples selected of the three stories show a relative consistency in the number of words used and the level as shown by the Fry Graph of reading difficulty.

Discussion

Watson's writing style is somewhat revealed by the listing of the word count of all fifty-six short stories and four novels by Professor Lauterbach. In a tabulation recorded by Professor Lauterbach showed that the total number of words written in the stories from 1890-1909 is 336, 490 in the 39 cases. The period from 1910-1927 indicated that a word count is 119,704 with 17 cases, an average of 7,041 words. He concluded that shorter stories appeared during this latter period. Some might equate length of texts to its readability, perhaps shorter stories are easier to complete. However, it is not the length of the story but the type of specialized and technical vocabulary used that may either increase or decrease ease of comprehension.

Further comparisons are demonstrated applying a readability formula on randomly selected passages from five stories; three written by Dr. Watson and two by Holmes. Sentence length, word count, and number of syllables are fairly consistent across the passages. Variability in sentence length was accounted for by sampling additional randomly selected passages.

Readability formulas and word lists used to measure ease or difficulty of text difficulty can be manipulated. If the sentences are short and the words used contain fewer syllables per word, a passage can be reported at a certain readability level, when in essence, it may be more difficult to understand in a meaningful manner. For example, "The Red-Headed League" is a story read by adolescents that appears in English literature texts. A simple sentence appearing in this story is, "There is the first volume of it in the press." Now if we apply the formula to this sentence it is rather benign since the sentence length and syllable count is minimal. However, what is not taken into consideration in this formula is the one syllable word "press" that may cause confusion for a reader with its meaning in this context as a shelved cupboard, or case. Thus, this sample sentence might score well for ease of reading, but it actually could challenge comprehension.

A caution is repeated that a readability formula provides an "estimate" of passage difficulty. As noted above, the scores on 3 passages can vary depending on word choice or sentence complexity. Formulas should not be used as sole determiners when matching a Sherlock Holmes story with an individual. Factors not measured by readability formulas are presented to emphasize that their consideration is significant. Other important factors that override readability formulas are a reader's purpose, interest, motivation, and prior knowledge with the content that is to be read.

A question that can only be answered by the reader is, "Who is the better story-teller, Watson or Holmes?" Why?

Sherlock Holmes Encounters Three Professors

There is no one more easy to trace than a schoolmaster.
There are scholastic agencies by which one may identify
any man who has been in the profession.

(*The Hound of the Baskervilles*)

Sherlock Holmes encounters three professors; each with a differing set of personalities, dispositions, and circumstances. One an invalid confined for the most part to his bed surrounded by books and cigarette smoke. Another obsessed with finding the serum for returning to one's youth. A third, brilliant; but yet, cunning and unkind. My fascination led me to analyze how professors are treated in the Canon. I examined how these professors reveal their personalities, dispositions, and the circumstances in which they are portrayed in their respective stories.

Professor James Moriarty

Dr. Watson provides some insight of Professor Moriarty in four stories: *The Valley of Fear, The Final Problem, The Adventure of the Empty House, and The Norwood Builder*. In passing, he is mentioned in two other stories, *His Last Bow* and *The Adventure of the Illustrious Client*.

It is Sherlock Holmes who provides the description of Professor Moriatry's personality, his disposition toward being an unkind soul, and couches the circumstances into criminal behavior by calling him, "The Napoleon of Crime."

"He is the Napoleon of crime, Watson. He is the organizer of half that
is evil and of nearly all that is undetected in this great city. He is a
genius, a philosopher, an abstract thinker. He has a brain of the first
order. He sits motionless, like a spider in the centre of its web, but

that web has a thousand radiations, and he knows well every quiver
of each of them. He does little himself. He only plans. But his agents
are numerous and splendidly organized. Is there a crime to be done,
a paper to be abstracted, we will say, a house to be rifled, a man to be
removed - the word is passed to the Professor, the matter is organized
and carried out." (*The Final Problem*)

It is this paragraph that provides a clear image of the professor's knowledge,
reasoning ability, cunning, and willingness to do evil rather than direct these talents for
the betterment of society. There is no mistaking that Professor Moriarty is compared to
Napoleon Bonaparte. For Watson sees Moriarty as having the same personal
characteristics as those possessed by Napoleon. It is interesting to compare the deeds of
Professor Moriarty to those of Napoleon during his reign in France.

We are told in *The Valley of Fear* that Professor Moriarty in addition to the
aforementioned description, once again enumerated, that he is a brilliant mathematician.
Although he is shrouded from the public in his criminal endeavors he is revered for his
knowledge of applied mathematics as evidenced in his book, "The Dynamics of an
Asteroid." It is this public trait that he is known of his intellect by his fellow
mathematicians.

"Is he not the celebrated author of The Dynamics of an Asteroid - a book which
ascends to such rarefied heights of pure mathematics that it is said that there was
no man in the scientific press capable of criticizing it?

(*The Valley of Fear*)

The Professor's public knowledge is further revealed by Holmes in *The Final
Problem*. We learn that Professor Moriarty is well-born and has received an excellent
education bolstered by his superior intellect in mathematics. At age twenty-one he writes
a treatise upon the Binomial Theorem which establishes him within the European
academic community. As a result of this treatise he is given a chair in mathematics at an
unnamed university. Despite these accomplishments, Professor Moriarty falls from the
good graces of the university fellows and takes on his underworld mission. Sherlock
Holmes describes this demise:

'But the man had hereditary tendencies of the most diabolical kind. A criminal
strain ran in his blood, which, instead of being modified, was increased and
rendered infinitely more dangerous by his extraordinary mental powers. Dark
rumours gathered round him in the university town, and eventually he was
compelled to resign his Chair and to come down to London, where he set up

as an army coach."

(*The Final Problem*).

Just as Sherlock Holmes observes Professor Moriarty, Watson tells us that Professor Moriarty has been keeping watch over Holmes' activities. It is during the visit of the Professor to the lodgings of Sherlock Holmes that he reveals this series of undertakings.

> `On the 23rd you incommoded me; by the middle of February I was seriously inconvenienced by you; at the end of March I was absolutely hampered in my plans; and now, at the close of April, I find myself placed in such a position through your continual persecution that I am in positive danger of losing my liberty. The situation is becoming an impossible one.'

(*The Final Problem*)

Professor Moriarty makes his threat apparent by having Holmes stampeded by a horse drawn van.

> "My dear Watson, Professor Moriarty is not a man who lets the grass grow under his feet. I went out about midday to transact some business in Oxford Street. As I passed the corner which leads from Bentinck Street on to the Welbeck Street crossing a two-horse van furiously driven whizzed round and was on me like a flash. I sprang for the footpath and saved myself by the fraction of a second. The van dashed round from Marylebone Lane and was gone in an instant.

(*The Final Problem*).

It is this incident that leads to the demise of Professor Moriarty and the resurrection of Sherlock Holmes at Richenbach Falls. Just when we think that Watson has relieved us from the Professor he emerges again in spirit through his colleague and chief-of-staff, Colonel Sebastian Moran who makes a failed attempt on Sherlock Holmes' life with an air gun.

Professor Presbury

Professor Presbury makes his appearance in Watson's writing of *The Adventure of the Creeping Man*. Like Professor Moriarty and Professor Coram, a university affiliation is attributed to Professor Presbury. Watson writes that it is Holmes that wishes this story to be told:

> If only to dispel once for all the ugly rumours which some twenty years ago agitated the University and were echoed in the learned societies of London.

> *(The Adventure of the Creeping Man)*.

There are many instances in the stories of the Canon where Holmes stresses the importance of education. However, it is clear that Holmes, through Watson, doesn't want the "University" to be degraded or perceived as less than a place of higher learning by the misdeeds of some faculty. For it is the university setting and education, itself, that is the beacon of light for students to become self-educating (*The Naval Treaty*, *The Red Circle*).

A reading of this story provides another insight into the personality, disposition, and the circumstances under which Professor Presbury is driven towards reclaiming his youthful physical characteristics. Watson provides us with an intriguing question, "Why does Professor Presbury's faithful wolf-hound, Roy, endeavour to bite him?" It is Holmes who takes the challenge by providing an answer. Unlike professors with whom I am acquainted, Professor Presbury is wealthy. We know that Professor Presbury is sixty-one years of age, is a faculty member in the department of Comparative Anatomy, and is vainly, even showing a "passionate frenzy," to find a way to recapture the physical attributes he once possessed. However, it is in his desire to capture the heart of a younger woman that his passion for youth becomes an obsession. So much so, that he begins to draw the attention of other faculty members and associates, one of whom is his secretary, Mr. Bennett.

His personality changes by becoming "furtive and sly." So too, does his disposition when Mr. Bennett reveals to Holmes that "he was not the man that they had known, but that he was under some shadow which had darkened his higher qualities…. Always there was something new, something sinister and unexpected." We now wait for Watson to develop these unusual characteristics and he does by relating what Mr. Bennett has to say about Professor Presbury:

> "I saw that it was he. He was crawling, Mr. Holmes - crawling! He was not quite on his hands and knees. I should rather say on his hands and feet, with his face

sunk between his hands. Yet he seemed to move with ease. I was so paralysed by the sight that it was not until he had reached my door that I was able to step forward and ask if I could assist him. His answer was extraordinary. He sprang up, spat out some atrocious word at me, and hurried on past me and down the staircase."

Without doubt, Professor Presbury exhibits extraordinary traits that emphasize how one's transition in personality, disposition, and existing circumstances can be dramatically displayed. The answer to the question of the dog is revealed by Holmes. Suffice it to say, "The dog, of course, was aware of the change far more quickly than you [Mr. Bennett]."

Professor Coram

We learn in *The Golden Pince-Nez*, that Professor Coram is well-liked by his neighbors, that he surrounds himself with books, and like the other two professors had been a professor at an unnamed university. In this case, a Russian University.

The circumstances to which is he depicted is that of an invalid who is wheeled around in a bath chair, uses a stick to "hobble" around the house, and is confined mostly to a bed where he is enthralled in working on a learned book. His disposition is one that is oriented toward habitually smoking Alexandrian cigarettes. So much so, that they become the clue to solving the mystery. Very little is known about his personality other than he was "buried in his work, and existed for nothing else." He must have kept to himself due to his incapacitation of health and movement. It may be surmised that his conversations were restricted since he was devoted to reading books and also preoccupied with the one he was writing.

He did have a sinister side to his personality as evidenced by his wife, Anna's exclamation:

"Why should you cling so hard to that wretched life of yours, Sergius?" said she.

"It has done harm to many and good to none - not even to yourself... My husband betrayed his own wife and his companions. Yes, we were all arrested upon his confession. Some of us found our way to the gallows and some to Siberia."

Watson is less inclined to represent the inner traits of Professor Coram compared to those of Professor Moriarty and Professor Presbury. Although the circumstances surrounding the events relate to Professor Coram, he serves more as a foil even though a culprit in the development and solving of this mystery.

Discussion

Watson, not to be confused with A. Conan Doyle his literary agent, although the writing styles are quite similar, reveals interesting comparisons and contrasts when examining the three stories featuring the professors. Each of the three professors is portrayed differently when compared to personality, disposition, and circumstance. Professor Moriarty is sinister, evil, and ruthless. He is inclined to be overly predisposed toward controlling London's underworld activities. His physical characteristics are described as reptilian, but his knowledge of mathematics is unequaled. The circumstances to which he is positioned is one who lurks in the shadows; capable of carrying-out horrific deeds.

Professor Presbury and Professor Coram are unlike Professor Moriarty. Professor Presbury is on an unrealistic quest to capture his youth for a younger woman, and relies on serums that drastically change his personality and disposition, not withstanding his physical changes. Only Professor Coram is shrouded in revealing his personality. We gain some insight into his past endeavors, but the focus is not on him as an individual but rather the circumstances that lead to solving the mystery. Once it is solved, we are privy to more of his past as presented by his wife, Anna.

In this essay, I examined how professors are portrayed in the Canon – their personalities, their dispositions, and situated actions. In the next essay, I take the professor theme further by arguing that Sherlock Holmes could have been a professor after his retirement.

Sherlock Holmes As College Professor[23]

"He propped his test-tube in the rack, and began to
lecture with the air of a professor addressing his class."

(The Adventure of the Dancing Men)

Sherlock Holmes reminisces about his lonely time spent at his home in Sussex. He mentions little contact with Watson other than an "occasional week-end visit."[24] It is during this period that I speculate that Sherlock Holmes becomes a visiting professor in Cambridge at Sidney Sussex College for short intervals. Although enjoying his avocation of tending to the bees, his vocation of detection along with its encompassing attributes encroaches upon his idleness and spurs him to share his knowledge with others.

When one speaks of the professor and Sherlock Holmes the sinister image of Professor Moriarty quickly comes to mind with the vivid portrait of the struggle at Reichenbach Falls in Switzerland. However, my daily encounters with professors at a university negate this foreboding image; however, students may disagree. It is clear that Watson sees Holmes in a professorial state.[25] Of more import, Holmes portrays himself in the image of a professor. He demonstrates his knowledge of the subject matter, conducts research, reduces complex events so that others can understand his reasoning processes, publishes papers, monographs, and books, and engages others using the Socratic method in solving cases.

Scholarly Pursuits

"Shall the examination proceed?" "Yes, let it proceed, by all means."

- The Three Students

A casual reading of the great detective's methods conveys his extensive knowledge of chemistry and the chemical problems in which he is confronted during his investigations. The chronicles illustrate detailed examples of his use of scientific knowledge to solve complex problems. His dwelling at 221B Baker Street contains the

---

[23] A shorter version of this essay appeared as Marino C. Alvarez, "Sherlock Holmes As College Professor." *Baker Street Journal*, vol. 51, no. 1, (Spring, 2001): 44-48. Reprinted with the kind permission of *The Baker Street Journal*.
[24] *The Adventure of the Lion's Mane.*
[25] Refer to quotation introducing this section taken from *"The Adventure of the Dancing Men."*

chemical desk and chemical paraphernalia in the corner of the living room.[26] Both Dr. Watson and Mrs. Hudson comment on the odors that are sometimes present in the dwelling.[27]

He is frequently preoccupied with chemical experiments that occupy his thoughts without regard to time or the effect of the gases that fill the apartment:

> He [Holmes] would hardly reply to my questions and busied himself
>
> all the evening in an abstruse chemical analysis, which involved much
>
> heating of retorts and distilling of vapors, ending at last in a smell
>
> which fairly drove me out of the apartment. Up to the small hours
>
> of the morning I could hear the clinking of his test-tubes which told
>
> me that he was still engaged in his malodorous experiments.
>
> *- The Sign of the Four*

Again we are privy to his untiring efforts when engaged in chemical experiments, as Watson recounts a telegram that comes late in the evening just when he is about to retire for the evening. Holmes is deeply involved with an experiment:

> Holmes was settling down to one of those all-night chemical
>
> researches which he frequently indulged in, when I would leave
>
> him stooping over a retort and a test-tube at night, and find him
>
> in the same position when I came down to breakfast in the morning.
>
> *- The Adventure of the Copper Beaches*

His chemical investigations include both basic and applied research. Many of his chemical experiments are applied to his cases. However there are times that he engages in chemical research studies that are classified as basic research, the discovery of new information. To engage in basic research was novel since there were few chemists who conducted basic chemical experiments during that period.[28] For example, in *A Study in*

---

[26] *The Adventure of the Mazarin Stone* and *The Adventure of the Empty House.*

[27] See Dr. Watson's comments in *The Sign of the Four, The Adventure of the Dancing Men,* and *The Adventure of the Dying Detective.*

[28] Edward J. Van Liere, *A Doctor Enjoys Sherlock Holmes* (New York: Vantage Press, 1959), 75.

Scarlet, Holmes conducts an experiment and discovers a method for blood identification in humans. He exclaims, "Now we have the Sherlock Holmes' test...."[29]

A glimpse into his days as a college student reveals his devotion to learning in the areas of science and literature. His college undergraduate days foreshadow his demeanor, attention to detail, use of imagination, determination, quick-wit, and time given to scholarly pursuits.

College Days

As a college student, Holmes engaged in rigorous study.[30] He tells us that he "spent seven weeks working out a few experiments in organic chemistry."[31] His scholarly pursuits seemed to be fueled more by his interests rather than by his tutors.

---

[29] When first introduced to Watson by Stamford, Holmes is engaged in a significant discovery. "The question now is about haemoglobin.... It is interesting, chemically, no doubt [Watson says]...but practically---." Holmes exclaims, "it is the most practical medico-legal discovery for years. Don't you see that it gives us an infallible test for blood stains?" He then engages both Watson and Stamford in teaching them what he has discovered and the practical implications it has in criminal investigations (*A Study in Scarlet*).

[30] There is disagreement about the college Sherlock Holmes attended. Many scholarly articles have been written advocating for either Cambridge or Oxford. O.F. Grazebrook's well-written book suggests Oxford as the college, *Studies in Sherlock Holmes 1. Oxford or Cambridge*. Printed in Great Britain for Private Circulation by Ebenezer Baylis and Sons, (Worcester and London: The Trinity Press); Nicholas Utechin favors St. Johns College at Oxford, "This Charming Town: Sherlock Holmes at Oxford," *Baker Street Journal*, vol. 26, no. 3., (September, 1976), 135-140; Christopher Morley, "Was Sherlock Holmes an American?" using Sydney Paget's rendering of Holmes with a light blue ribbon, places him in Cambridge; Dorothy Sayers, "Holmes' College Career," *Unpopular Opinions* (London: Victor Gollancz, 1946, and Bernard Darwin, "Sherlockiana: The Faith of a Fundamentalist." In J.E. Holroyd, *Seventeen Steps to 221B*. (London: George Allen & Unwin ltd., 1967), have Holmes at Cambridge. Professor R.J. Chorley writes of Holmes as an undergraduate student at Sidney Sussex College Cambridge during the years 1871-1873, *Sherlock Holmes at Sidney Sussex College 1871-1873: An Imaginative Reconstruction,* 1997. William S. Baring-Gould states that Holmes first attended Christ Church College in Oxford where he meets Victor Trevor, and then attends Cambridge: Gonville and Caius College, *Sherlock Holmes of Baker Street* (New York: Bramhall House, Chapter, Oxford and Cambridge: 1872-77, 1962), 25-33. In *The Missing Three-Quarter* the university named is in Cambridge, however, Holmes makes no reference to ever attending. Likewise, in *The Three Students*, the college is St. Luke's but the university is not named. Darwin places this college in Cambridge based on Watson's description of the tutor's room looking on to "the ancient lichen-tinted Court." He notes, however, that Holmes' statement, "We will take a walk in the Quadrangle" points to Oxford.

[31] *The Gloria Scott*.

Times spent conducting these experiments provided little for socialization among his fellow-students. Classmates perceived him as a loner with few acquaintances. However Holmes was an individualist who was more interested in making his college experience meaningful for him rather than being molded into a subset of learning about prescribed outcomes. His challenges come when faced with using his imagination and applying new learning to problem-oriented tasks.

It is during this period when he realizes that his powers of deduction can be used to notice the actions of others, but for aiding those in distress. These powers are aided by his studious endeavors in the fields of science, literature, mathematics, music, and art.

During this time Holmes reads a variety of books in the fields of philosophy, literature, science, mathematics, and history, concentrating especially on those passages that dealt with scientific and deductive reasoning.[32] It is my belief that Voltaire, although not mentioned in the Canon, was one of these writers that he read. To illustrate, the science of deductive reasoning can be found in the writings of Voltaire (1964, see pp. 28-31) in 1747.[33] In chapter three, Zadig deduces that a lost dog, which he has never seen, is not a dog (a male canine). "It is a little Spaniel bitch...." "She has recently had puppies, she limps in the left foreleg, and her ears are very long." Zadig explains his deductive reasoning. While walking in the woods, he discerns dog tracks in the sand; that it is a female from the "furrows, traced in the sand" between paw prints that indicated "a bitch with hanging dugs, which must therefore have had puppies a few days before." The long ears were discerned from the tracks that "brushed the sand at either side of the forefeet," and the lameness from the impression of the sand being more indented "by one paw than by the other three." Voltaire, through Zadig, in this episode also describes the physical features of a lost horse using deductive reasoning.

Prompted by Voltaire's portrayal of Zadig's deduction, Holmes developed a keen sense whenever a dog was present in his cases. An analogy can be made to Holmes' astute awareness of the presence of dogs in his later cases (e.g., *The Hound of the Baskervilles, Silver Blaze, and Lion's Mane*). So much is this apparent that in 1903 Holmes mentions his intention to write a monograph entitled *Upon the Uses of Dogs in the Work of the Detective*. Unfortunately, there is no report by Watson of its publication.[34]

---

[32] See Madeleine B. Stern, *Sherlock Holmes: Rare Book Collector. With a New Introduction and Short-Title Catalogue of The Sherlock Holmes Library*, (Paulette Greene: Rockville Centre, New York, 1981).
[33] Voltaire. *Zadig/L'ingenu* (New York: Penguin Books, 1964). Originally written in 1747. Translated by John Butt.
[34] *The Adventure of the Creeping Man.*

I further believe that soon after Holmes left college he could not miss the opportunity to read "A Piece of Chalk," by T. H. Huxley.[35] Huxley in a lecture to workingmen discusses the geological components of the earth's surface through the use of chalk. The essay is particularly noteworthy for he describes an experiment to determine the compounds of chalk: carbonic acid and quicklime (see p. 177). He further explains circumstances where chalk has been found and reveals other interesting facts in which chalk is an important substance for documenting our geological history by making scientific deductions of the world's surface in prehuman times. Watson quoting from "*The Book of Life*" written by Sherlock Holmes, states, "From a drop of water...a logician could infer the possibility of an Atlantic or a Niagara without having seen or heard of one or the other. So all life is a great chain, the nature of which is known whenever we are shown a single link of it."[36] Just as Huxley (1883) applies deductive reasoning to prehistoric times, so does Holmes use it to reconstruct mysterious events surrounding his cases.

Consulting Days

It is during his time as a consulting detective that Holmes continues his readings, writings and scientific experimentations, and pursues his love of the theater and music. References to each of these endeavors are replete throughout the Canon. In *The Adventure of the Lion's Mane* we are told of his passion for reading, "I am an omnivorous reader." His Baker Street lodgings have an array of "old books" where he would spend many happy hours reading them.[37]

There are a substantial number of references in the Canon that demonstrate the extensive literary knowledge of Sherlock Holmes. Upon describing to Watson his reasoning processes in solving *The Case of the Red Headed League*, Watson responds, "You reasoned it out beautifully." Holmes replies, "My life is spent in one long effort to escape from the commonplaces of existence. These little problems help me to do so." Watson counters, "And you are the benefactor of the race." Holmes shrugs and quotes from a letter of Gustave Flaubert (a French novelist and author of *Madame Bovary*) to George Sand, "L'homme c'est rien---l'oeuvre c'est tout" (Man is nothing---work is everything.)

A telling moment in *The Boscombe Valley Mystery* describes how Holmes clears his mind by delving into literature. When recapping events to Watson, he calls his attention to two "crucial" points, which he describes. Upon finishing he closes this discussion by

---

[35] T. H. Huxley, *Lay Sermons, Addresses, and Reviews* (London: Macmillan and Company, 1883).
[36] *A Study in Scarlet*.
[37] *A Scandal in Bohemia*.

saying, "And now let us talk about George Meredith [an English poet and novelist, 1828-1909], if you please, and we shall leave all minor matters until tomorrow." His escape to literary works is again demonstrated earlier in this same episode while travelling on the train with Watson. After reading several newspapers he selects the local Herefordshire paper, points to a paragraph, and asks Watson to read about the evidence given by Mr. James McCarthy. Following a brief discussion of the events, Holmes says to Watson, "No sir, I shall approach this case from the point of view that what this young man says is true, and we shall see whither that hypothesis will lead us." He then tells Watson, "And now here is my pocket Petrarch, and not another word shall I say of this case until we are on the scene of action."[38]

Holmes shows his knowledge of an American writer, Henry David Thoreau (1817-1862), author of Walden, in *The Adventure of the Noble Bachelor*.[39] In his journal entry for November 11, 1854, Thoreau writes, "Some circumstantial evidence is very strong, as when you find a trout in the milk." Holmes refers to Thoreau's example and uses this quote when explaining to Watson how his conjecture evolves into certainty, "Circumstantial evidence is occasionally very convincing, as when you find a trout in the milk."

His knowledge of science and literature is tempered by his appreciation of music. Many an evening is spent playing his violin as he mediates on problems of interest. Watson remarks that Holmes is not only an "enthusiastic musician…very capable…but a composer of no ordinary merit."[40] His appreciation and knowledge of music spur his prowess as a musician. It is during his investigation of Jabez Wilson that he asks Watson to accompany him to a concert at St. James Hall. "Sarasate plays at the St. James Hall this afternoon."[41] Pablo de Sarasate was a prominent violinist and composer from Pamplona in northern Spain.[42] Holmes also enjoyed the opera. He specifically mentions Richard Wagner (1813-1883) and asks Watson to accompany him to Covent Garden to catch "the second act."[43]

---

[38] Petrarch (1304-1374) was a notable Italian poet, scholar, and humanist who wrote in both Italian and Latin.

[39] Thoreau was an American essayist, poet, and naturalist.

[40] *The Red Headed League.*

[41] *Ibid.*

[42] Pablo de Sarasate (1844-1908) was born in the city of Pamplona in northern Spain, and is one of its most famous sons. At the annual *Fiesta de San Fermin*, when the running of the bulls through the streets occurs, there is also another fiesta being celebrated in the vicinity of the music conservatory in honor of Pablo de Sarasate, violinist and composer.

[43] *The Red Circle.*

A Call to Academia

"Education never ends, Watson. "

- The Adventure of the Red Circle

In the *Final Problem* Holmes mentions that he has been well paid in his services to crowned heads and that he is thinking of retiring from business and taking to chemistry. My contention is that while living in Sussex a combination of circumstances prevailed that drew him to academia in Cambridge.

While at Baker Street he was confronted with problems that had promise for investigation. His curiosity drove him to test his scientific theories using critical and imaginative thought. He constantly longed for cases that would challenge his intellect. Idleness was a curse, and he drove himself, despite fatigue, to achieve distinction. He was fascinated with education both in his pursuit and desire to teach others.

Sherlock Holmes' passion for education is clearly expressed to Watson upon reentering London through Clapham Junction:

> Holmes was sunk in profound thought, and hardly opened his eyes until
> we had passed Clapham Junction. "It's a very cheering thing to come
> into London by way of these lines which run high and allow you to look
> down upon the houses like this."
> I thought that he was joking, for the view was sordid enough, but he
> soon explained himself.
> "Look at those big, isolated clumps of buildings rising up above the slates,
> like brick islands in a lead-coloured sea"
> "The Board Schools."
> "Lighthouses, my boy! Beacons of the future! Capsules, with hundreds
> of bright little seeds in each, out of which will spring the wiser, better
> England of the future…."
> (*The Naval Treaty* – Doubleday edition, pp. 456-457)

Upon leaving Baker Street for the Sussex coast he lived a life of leisure. He became enthralled with the practice of bee keeping that kept him busy to an extent.

Being called into service when Fitzroy McPherson (a science master) is found dead at the edge of the cliff excites his mental faculties.[44] Soon after McPherson's dog, an Airedale terrier, is found in the same state of his master Holmes is prompted to search among his books for a particular one that contained specific information. After an hour he emerges with "a little chocolate and silver volume" that he eagerly scours for the chapter he remembered vaguely that contained "out of the way knowledge" pertinent to this case.

It is during this time I believe, that there are serious inquires into his availability to come to Sidney Sussex College to teach a seminar on "The Role of Chemistry and Detection." Holmes has achieved fame through his scientific and deductive methods in America, Egypt, and France.[45] In fact, the French Surete names its crime laboratories in Lyons after him. His name is known throughout Europe causing his brother Mycroft to exclaim, "I hear of Sherlock everywhere...." His writings on the use of plaster of Paris for preserving clues, differentiating 140 forms of cigar, cigarette, and pipe tobacco ashes, and collecting dust samples to determine a person's occupation or his location are methods adopted throughout the world in police agencies.[46] I speculate that the Master of the College prevails upon him personally to share his wisdom with England's future.

And so, not long after Holmes solves *"The Case of the Lion's Mane,"* he is approached by an official of Sidney Sussex College asking him to return to Cambridge offering him a position as a Professor of Chemistry. Normally a Lectureship would be offered, but given Holmes' status the thought of such a proposition would be out of the question. Realizing that he yearns for stimulating thought that such a post could satisfy, he consents to accept on a provisional part-time basis rather than a full-term with the understanding that he may leave the classroom at a given moment when the "game is afoot."

Further, there is evidence to support the proposition that Sherlock Holmes accepts this invitation. First, there is an appeal to his concern about England's future. Second, there is an allure for him as educator to share his wisdom and promote students'

---

[44] *The Adventure of the Lion's Mane.*

[45] *The Greek Interpreter.*

[46] Vincent Strarret, *The Private Life of Sherlock Holmes* (Chicago: The University of Chicago Press, 1960), lists several writings that show Holmes' expertise with various aspects of detection. Examples include: Upon the Distinction between the Ashes of the Various Tobaccos (*Study in Scarlet, Sign of the Four, Boscombe Valley Mystery*). Upon the Tracing of Footsteps (*Sign of the Four*). Upon the Influence of a Trade upon the Form of the Hand. (*Sign of the Four*). On the Typewriter and Its Relation to Crime (*Case of Identity*). Of Tattoo Marks (*Red Headed League*). On Secret Writings (*Dancing Men*). On the Polyphonic Motets of Lassus. Printed for private circulation (*Bruce-Partington Plans*). Chaldean Roots in the Ancient Cornish Language (*Devil's Foot*).

problem-oriented learning under meaningful circumstances. His experience and wealth of knowledge, coupled with his desire to fuel the fires of students to pursue rigorous study, prompts him to accept the professorial post where he again can make his mark on England's future – this time in education.

The third is the opportunity to avail himself of the College's library and scientific laboratory. He views this as an excellent opportunity to complete his book on detection using the extensive collection of the library combined with his own recollections and scrapbook entries. It may be recalled that Holmes proposed to devote his declining years to the composition of his textbook, *The Whole Art of Detection*, which was to "focus the whole art of detection into one volume." He mentioned it to Watson on a cold morning in the winter of 1897.[47] Of course, there is also ample opportunity for him to complete two other works begun earlier: *Early English Charter*[48] and *Upon the Uses of Dogs in the Work of the Detective*.[49]

It is not difficult to discern why Sherlock Holmes is sought after as a professor. He exhibits qualities that exemplify the best in a professor. He is insightful, curious, has an inquiring mind, seeks answers, is fair-minded, and is a critical and imaginative thinker.[50] His students have been heard to say that "Professor Holmes is often direct and exercises little patience. "Sometimes he is blunt and to the point." They say that he is at his best when using the Socratic method of teaching.[51] However, they are quick to add that preparing for his lectures require considerable study.

Conclusion

"I play the game for the game's own sake"

- The Adventure of the Bruce-Partington Plans

---

[47] *The Adventure of the Abbey Grange.*
[48] *The Three Students.*
[49] *The Adventure of the Creeping Man.*
[50] Holmes describes the ideal reasoner as a person when "once [has] been shown a single fact in all its bearings, deduce from it not only all the chain of events which led up to it but also all the results which would follow from it" (*The Five Orange Pips*). He alludes to the writings of Cuvier who could, from the identification of one bone, construct a chronology of its links past and present.
[51] The reader may recall instances in which Holmes often asks Watson what he makes of the circumstances surrounding the events of a case. Watson is presented with probing questions that are intended for him to search his mind and assemble reasonable inferences.

At the College there are times when he can be observed attending concerts in the Cambridge area. The music from the strings of his violin can sometimes be heard during the early evening hours in the College's Music Conservatory. Across from the Master's Lodge in the Garden several beehives have mysteriously appeared. There are reported sightings of a man that dutifully cares for them; however, he is difficult to recognize because of the meshed head covering and long coat. A student walking along the path near the beehives mentioned to some of his fellow classmates that he passed a gentlemen dressed for the tending of the bees. In his gloved hand he noticed a book entitled *Practical Handbook of Bee Culture, with Some Observations upon the Segregation of the Queen*.[52]

He is often seen in the College's scientific library, located alongside the Master's Lodge, surrounded by papers, books and foolscap for taking notes. There is little doubt among his colleagues that he is completing unfinished works. At other times he is found working alone in the Chemistry Laboratory hunched over a chemical bench with test tubes radiating many colors with gases rising into the air. His fingers are often stained with acids, alkalies, silver nitrate, and other potent chemicals. Beside him lies a learned treatise that he occasionally scans on the chemistry of the alkaloids.[53] He engages his keen mind with many interesting chemical experiments using his intellect and imagination to their fullest.

During the late afternoon, when the long shadows sprawl across the garden lawn, his presence is noted at the Faculty Club alone in a special room designated to him by the Master of the College. Often he escapes into a literary work of interest with smoke leisurely flowing from his pipe toward the high ceiling. On rare occasions, a person unknown to the faculty or staff of the Faculty Club visits him. It is speculated that these persons come to him as clients to consult on matters of importance and sensitivity. Upon their departure, Renton, the resident attendant, has often observed him sitting in a comfortable chair with his eyes closed and his finger tips joined together. However, there was the time when Professor Nicholas Weatherby, who seemed to be in a state over "A Missing Manuscript," consulted with Sherlock Holmes. Renton remembers that Mr. Holmes remained long after closing hours. So long, in fact, that it necessitated the filling of his pipe three times.

---

[52] This book is mentioned in *His Last Bow*.
[53] Edward J. Van Liere, *A Doctor Enjoys Sherlock Holmes* (New York: Vantage Press, 1959) gives this description, although in a different setting, in his essay "Sherlock Holmes, The Chemist," 76.

Sherlock Holmes as Detective and Scientist

The world is full of obvious things which nobody
by any chance ever observes."

(*The Hound of the Baskervilles*)

Sherlock Holmes is revered as a consulting detective; however his pursuits involve him within the realm of a scientist. This essay provides a context for Sherlock Holmes' prowess as a detective based on his knowledge and experimentation with science. In so doing, cases are presented with the intent of exposing novice readers, especially adolescents, to the writings of the Canon using examples from formal schooling and societal environments. Of course, some of these bits and pieces can serve to initiate some deductive and scientific endeavors as we study the Canon. I draw from two articles that I have written in preparing this essay. One a research study, appearing in *Reading Research and Instruction*, where I compare and contrast a detective (Sherlock Holmes) with a scientist and use passages from *The Adventure of the Dancing Men*; the another, where I include Sherlock Holmes and some of his cases for high school students to engage in cross-disciplinary studies.[54]

Introduction

Reasoning in school is different from reasoning in real-world settings.[55] School-related problems are often prepared for students to solve in ways that do not necessarily apply to real-world problems. Real problems demand innovative reasoning that focuses on how the real world operates. Students need to be confronted with problem situations that relate in-school theoretical knowledge (thought) to out-of-school practical knowledge (action). The role of imaginative literature is a powerful influence in

---

[54] Marino C. Alvarez, & Risko, V.J. "Using a Thematic Organizer to Facilitate Transfer Learning with College Developmental Studies Students. *Reading Research and Instruction*, 28, 2, 1989, 1-15; Marino C. Alvarez. "The Reader as a Sleuth: Engagement by Intrusion." In N.D. Padak, T.V. Rasinski, & J. Logan, (Eds.), *Literacy research and practice: Foundations for the year 2000*, Fourteenth Yearbook of the College Reading Association (Pittsburg, KS: College Reading Association, 1992), 101-108.

[55] H.G. Petrie. Interdisciplinary education: Are we faced with insurmountable opportunities? In G. Grant (Ed.), *Review of Research in Education*, Vol. 18 (Washington, DC: American Educational Research Association, 1992), 299-333.; also, R. Roy. Interdisciplinary Science on Campus: The Elusive Dream. In J. Kockelmans (Ed.), *Interdisciplinary and Higher Education* (University Park: Pennsylvania State University Press, 1979), 161-196.

intellectual development.[56] As one reads a novel, a certain degree of reflective thinking and repositioning is incurred as hypotheses are formulated and meanings reconstructed. Some argue that this reformulation occurs more frequently in detective stories.[57] This reformulation of events in detective novels requires an understanding of in-school theoretical knowledge and practical knowledge of real world situations. The notion that thought and action work in close proximity, Petrie argues, is a way in which the disciplines are used in an integrative fashion as a means of solving practical problems that include ways of thinking about these disciplines.[58] Formulating connections between events and objects among disciplines in formal settings is one way for enhancing conceptual understanding of real problems confronting society.

We have opportunities to relate what we see and hear to what we read. While visiting a high school, I saw an outline of a body sketched on the floor with masking tape in the hallway. I asked the significance of this outline to passing students. One student replied, "There is none. The seniors just did it." With a little imagination by the mathematics teacher, however, such an outline can be related to the many situations described in detective fiction as well as to those same images projected in television shows and movies. Mathematical problems can be developed using this body outline to obtain the height, weight, position angles, and so forth.

Observing the body outline and finding a purpose for its being can be a powerful intrusion into making connections between events that happen in narratives and those that can be applied to real-life applications of learned principles in mathematics, history, science, business education, music, art, health education, home economics, and technology. This intermingling of narrative and expository discourse across disciplines

---

[56]Robert Coles, *The Call of Stories: Teaching and the Moral Imagination* (Boston: Houghton Mifflin, 1989); also, Marilyn G. Eanet, Expanding Literacy By the Use of Imaginative Literature in the Teacher Education Classroom. In B.L. Hayes & K. Camperell (Eds.), *Literacy: International, National, State, and Local*. Eleventh Yearbook of the American Reading Forum (Logan, UT: Utah State University, 1991), 57-66.
Eanet, M.G. (1991). Expanding literacy by the use of imaginative literature in the teacher education classroom. In B.L. Hayes & K. Camperell (Eds.), *Literacy: International, national, state, and local*. Eleventh Yearbook of the American Reading Forum (pp. 57-66). Logan, UT: Utah State University.
[57] For example, see D. Porter. *The Pursuit of Crime: Art and Ideology in Detective Fiction*. (New Haven, CT: Yale University Press, 1981).
[58] H.G. Petrie. Interdisciplinary Education: "Are We Faced with Insurmountable Opportunities?" In G. Grant (Ed.), *Review of Research in Education*, Vol. 18 (Washington, DC: American Educational Research Association, 1992), 299-333.

requires knowledge activation, critical thinking, and schema construction to occur within students.[59]

Detectives and Scientists

When reading the Canon, the reader becomes the juror of the presentation of the evidence and the authenticity of the thought processes, methods, and conclusions reached by Holmes. The same traits exhibited by Holmes can be attributed to both detectives and scientists with some differences. Detectives and scientists are primarily concerned with the causes of the events and rely on observation to gather evidence. Detectives look for clues and investigate events surrounding a case; scientists use interviews and tests. Detectives and scientists form hypotheses based on their prior knowledge about the cause of the events and rule out those that are unreasonable. Both detectives and scientists tend to be extremely cautious about their conclusions for similar reasons. Their conclusions must withstand critical scrutiny of a jury of peers or a court of law. An important difference between detectives and scientists is in the way they form and use generalizations. Scientists are concerned with arriving at general statements that allow grouping of apparently dissimilar events under a single rule or generalization. Detectives are more interested in solving their cases rather than in establishing generalizations that might be produced from their work.

Sherlock Holmes combines the traits of a detective and a scientist as he contemplates the shroud that surrounds a particular problem or circumstance. However, he does not shun the use of generalization as does a typical detective. Holmes does use tests in his criminal investigations as evidenced in his long enduring experiments, and he conducts interviews and makes generalizations to related circumstances in his cases.

In a study we conducted with college developmental studies students to facilitate transfer learning using a thematic organizer, we investigated whether an instructional strategy could facilitate generalizability of ideas from one context to another.[60] A text adjunct, called a thematic organizer, was developed to activate students' prior knowledge and illustrate that attributes of a concept may differ when it is presented in two different contexts. I developed the thematic organizer as a text adjunct to help students' preview text information and generate connections between their prior

---

[59]Marino C. Alvarez, "Imaginative Uuses of Self-Selected Cases," *Reading Research and Instruction, vol. 32*, no. 2, 1993, 1-18; Marino C. Alvarez and Victoria J. Risko, "Using a Thematic Organizer to Facilitate Transfer Learning with College Developmental Studies Students." *Reading Research and Instruction*, vol.28, no. 2, 1989, 1-15; G.R. Potts, M.F. St. John & D. Kirson, "Incorporating New Information Into Existing World Knowledge," *Cognitive Psychology*. Vol. 21, 1989, 303-333, .
[60] Alvarez and Risko, 1989.

knowledge and text concepts (see Appendix A). More specifically, the thematic organizer is designed to: (1) highlight systematically and explicitly the central theme of the text; (2) relate the theme to experiences and/or knowledge that students already possess; (3) provide cohesion among the ideas to accommodate text structure; and, (4) aid schema construction by elaborating upon new and extended meanings of a thematic concept.[61] A thematic organizer differs from other types of *previews* in that it is developed to define and relate explicitly text themes through analogy to examples that are familiar to the reader.

The subjects were forty-eight low ability readers enrolled in college developmental studies classes. Materials included passages taken from a science and literature text, a thematic organizer, and a set of five open-ended questions. The findings indicated that the thematic strategy facilitated transfer learning. Further, the ordering of passage presentation according to structure did not affect comprehension differentially. This study suggests that low ability readers require an explicit explanation of the relationship between common elements of a concept that is presented in varied contexts and cannot rely on text structure alone to facilitate transfer of ideas.

Of direct interest in this writing is the literature passage, *The Adventures of the Dancing Men*. This passage consisted of 880 words that comprised the first two pages photocopied from the original text.[62] The literature passage contained examples of Holmes' deductive reasoning without explicit references to the term itself. For example, on the first page, Sherlock Holmes, to the amazement of Dr. Watson, is able to conclude accurately that Watson was not going to invest in South African securities. As Holmes explains how he knew what Watson was thinking, he identifies the clues that he followed to make his deductions. The strategy that he uses parallels the stages of deductive reasoning that are presented in the science passage that was used as a comparison. This introduction sets the stage for the main scenario and provides another example of how scientific reasoning is applied to solve the problem.

---

[61] See Marino C. Alvarez, "Using a thematic pre-organizer and guided instruction as aids to concept learning," *Reading Horizons*, 24, 1, 1983, 51-58; Marino C. Alvarez and Victoria J. Risko, "Using a thematic organizer to facilitate transfer learning with college developmental studies students," *Reading Research and Instruction*, 28, 2, 1989, 1-15; Marino C. Alvarez and Victoria J. Risko, Thematic Organizers. In B. J. Guzzetti. (Ed.), (*Literacy in America: An Encyclopedia of History, Theory, and Practice. Vols. I & II.* Santa Barbara, CA: ABC-CLIO, 2002), 653-655; and Victoria J. Risko and Marino C. Alvarez, "An investigation of poor readers' use of a thematic strategy to comprehend text. *Reading Research Quarterly*, vol. 21, no. 3, 1986, 298-316.
[62] Arthur Conan Doyle, *The Complete Sherlock Holmes* (Garden City, NY: Doubleday, 1905).

The thematic organizer written for *The Adventure of the Dancing Men* compared and contrasted a detective and a scientist in pursuing criminal and scientific outcomes (see Appendix A). The relevance of mentioning this study is twofold: One is that when reading the exploits of Sherlock Holmes it may add to our image of the similarities that are exhibited by him as both a detective and a scientist as he unravels his cases. Second, if we expect novice readers and adolescents to become interested with the Canon it may be necessary to provide them with explicit examples of how attributes of a concept can be generalized to varied situations in a context relevant to the readers' prior knowledge. Making these connections to introduce a Sherlock Holmes' story may pique their interest and provide them with an incentive to read these stories.

Making Connections Between the Past and Present Using Scientific Principles

Bridging the gap of the present and the past can be illustrated by the following two cases: comparing the typewriter with the computer and comparing Sherlock Holmes' blood identification test to present-day methods. The use of the typewriter keys as identifying marks in solving criminal cases had its beginnings in a Sherlock Holmes story (*A Case of Identity*). An individual's handwriting was compared to that of a typewriter typescript. "It is a curious thing…that a typewriter has really quite as much individuality as a man's handwriting….Some letters get more worn than others, and some wear only on one side."[63] This story was published in 1891, twenty-three years after the first practical typewriter was invented in 1868, and before such a technique was used in any actual case.[64] In fact, it prompts Sherlock to expound:

> "I think of writing another little monograph some of these days on the typewriter and its relation to crime. It is a subject to which I have devoted some little attention. I have here four letters which purport to come from the missing man. They are all typewritten. In each case, not only are the 'e's' slurred and the 'r's' tailless, but you will observe, if you care to use my magnifying lens, that the fourteen other characteristics to which I have alluded are there as well."

In 1992, I wrote that students can compare the events portrayed in this story to typewritten messages typed on personal or school typewriters or compare the type of letters and words to deduce fonts (e.g., roman, san script) and type of printer (e.g., dot

---

[63] Doyle, 1905, p. 199.
[64] H.J. Walls, H.J. "The Forensic Science Service in Great Britain: A Short History," *Forensic Science Society Journal*, vol. 16, 1976, 273-278.

matrix, laser).[65] This analysis can be conducted with messages typed and printed from various makes of typewriters, computers, and printers, using questions such as "Does the imprint of the letters signify letter differences as in the typewriter?" "Are there differences in the degree of impression made on a piece of paper by the keys of a typewriter when compared to a dot matrix or laser printer?" "Can you identify the kind of printer used in these messages?"

The implications of such a lesson apply to science that affects our everyday lives. For example, many of us are aware of how the forces of friction can wear metals, as in the impact of typewriter keys on the platen. This same principle can be applied to the use of the dot matrix versus the laser printer. Laying aside the differences in letter quality, we (students) may be interested how the FBI laboratory and state police crime laboratory are limited in their identification of laser printers but are presented with more data from a dot matrix printer. A dot matrix printer can be identified by make and individual machine due to the impressions made by the keys, unlike a laser printer that cannot be identified by individual machine because ink is sprayed on paper.

Another interesting case is the comparison of Sherlock Holmes' blood identification test to those used in present-day criminology (A Study in Scarlet). The analysis of blood stains is prominent in detective novels and television and movie portrayals. Although blood stains can be identified they cannot be attributed to a specific individual. A statement such as "This blood stain originated from that particular person" cannot be made since there is currently no method of assigning individuality to any particular person. However, the statement, "This blood stain did *not* originate from that particular person can be substantiated because characteristics of blood group systems and blood constituents have been identified and classified[66]

When ascertaining whether this statement still held today, I made inquires and through the efforts of Billy Fields was able to receive the following response from Tabitha A. Bullock, DNA Supervisor, Metropolitan Nashville Police Department.[67] She replied that the statement did, indeed, hold true when capabilities were limited to the technology of blood grouping and enzyme testing; however as DNA capabilities have

---

[65] Marino C. Alvarez, "The Reader as a Sleuth: Engagement by Intrusion. In N.D. Padak, T.V. Rasinski, & J. Logan, (Eds.), *Literacy Research and Practice*: Foundations for the Year 2000(Fourteenth Yearbook of the College Reading Association. Pittsburg, KS: College Reading Association, 1992), 101-108.

[66]C.G. Tedeschi, W.G. Eckert, & L.G. Tedeschi, (*Forensic Medicine: A Study in Trauma and Environmental Hazard (vol. II). Physical Trauma*. Philadelphia, PA: W.B. Saunders, 1977).

[67] When I wrote this piece, it was not known that such an analysis could be derived given the state of medical knowledge and technology at the time.

emerged and improved over the past 20 years, the accuracy of this statement has changed. She then described this updated process:

> The purpose of DNA technology is to determine the source of biological fluids such as bloodstains. DNA is used to analyze a bloodstain of unknown origin and determine the DNA profile of the blood. DNA profiles are also generated from samples collected directly from individuals, and are referred to as known or reference samples. The DNA profiles from unknown samples (i.e. blood, semen, saliva, vaginal discretion, skin cells, etc) can then be compared to the DNA profiles generated from reference samples. A report is then issued regarding the results of these comparisons. DNA reports may not use the exact wording: "This blood stain originated from that particular person;" however, DNA reports commonly state "The DNA profile obtained from the bloodstain matches the DNA profile obtained from Person X." Sometimes laboratories choose the words "consistent with" as opposed to "match." The caveat to reporting a "match" is that a statistic expressing "how common" the DNA profile is, is required. It is not uncommon for DNA statistics to reach 1 out of quadrillions or quintillions. When comparing statistics in the quadrillions or quintillions to a global population of around 6 billion, the statistical weight is significant.

> A number of DNA laboratories place more weight on a "match" with a high statistical value by making a statement such as: "To a degree of scientific certainty, excluding the existence of an identical twin, Person X is the source of the bloodstain." A statement such as this is considered an identity or source attribution statement. In my experience, this type of statement was made when random match probabilities exceeded 600 billion, approximately 100 times the world population. Some laboratories may set the bar lower than 600 billion, others may stick to a "match" statement regardless of how high the statistics reach.

In light of the sophistication of DNA blood analysis a look back into the historical period and what was known then about blood stains give us a retrospective view of how the procedure was done. This reflective stance is given by Sherlock Holmes in *A Study in Scarlet*.

An intriguing reading concerning the testing for blood stains is revealed in *A Study in Scarlet*. Watson first meets Holmes, who is engaged in an experiment that he is soon to discover as "an infallible test for blood stains."[68] Holmes mixes a drop of blood in a litre of water. Then he adds a "few white crystals" and "a few drops" of a transparent fluid. The contents of the beaker yields "a dull mahogany color, and a

---

[68] Doyle, 1905, 17-18.

brownish dust was precipitated to the bottom of the glass jar." Holmes compares this procedure to the guaiacum test that he calls "very clumsy and uncertain." He also dismisses the microscopic examination for blood corpuscles for the same reasons, especially if the blood stains have been allowed to set for hours before analysis.

This excerpt provides a thread for further investigation. A lesson on bloodstains can be developed that presents students with a reading of *A Study in Scarlet* and then compares the Sherlock Holmes test with those described by Samuel Gerber in *Chemistry and Crime*[69] where he shows the chemical bonds postulated by Holmes with those representations of other blood identification procedures[70] Students can then determine whether the procedures described in the story are credible given what was known about blood identification in 1875. This would lead them to make comparisons to present-day analyses and procedures[71]

Discussion

Stories within the Canon provide many opportunities for children and adolescents to become involved in "real" life experiments. The settings also elicit chances to delve into the historical, cultural, and political domains of the period. Artifacts such as original papers obtained in libraries and through online accesses; clothing worn; tools of the period, artistic and musical compositions; and, many others are ways to induce these young readers to interface narrative with informational texts. Actively engaging with a story's structural elements; in combination, with related activities using trade books, electronic texts, and primary sources that promote curiosity results in knowledge building, and also an appreciation for the literature and writing style of the Victorian era.

Keeping green the memory of Sherlock Holmes by using innovative teaching and learning methods is important. Developing an adjunct aid such as a thematic organizer to accompany a story's reading may be beneficial for activating background knowledge with the target concept of the story and also serve as a "mind set" for reading the story (see Appendix B). The interpretive statements guide the reader in becoming more of an

---

[69] S.M. Gerber, "A Study in Scarlet: Blood Identification in 1875. In S.M. Gerber (Ed.), *Chemistry and Crime: From Sherlock Holmes to Today's Courtroom* (Washington, DC: American Chemical Society, 1983), 31-35.
[70] See also, I. Asimov, "The Problem of the Blundering Chemist.," *Science Digest*, vol. 88,1980, 8-17; W.S. Baring-Gould, *Sherlock Holmes of Baker Street* (New York: Bramhall House, 1962).
[71] C.L. Huber, C.L. "The Sherlock Holmes Blood Test: The Solution to a Century-Old Mystery." In P.A. Shreffler (Ed.), *Sherlock Holmes by Gas-Lamp* (New York: Fordham University Press, 1989), 95-101; K. Simpson and B. Knight, *Forensic Medicine*. 9th ed.. (Baltimore: Edward Arnold, 1985).

active participant seeking deeper meaning with the characters, setting, plot, and theme of a story.

Appendix A

Thematic organizer developed to accompany the first two pages of *The Adventure of the Dancing Men* that appears in the article, Marino C. Alvarez and Victoria J. Risko. (1989). "Using a Thematic Organizer to Facilitate Transfer Learning with College Developmental Studies Students." *Reading Research and Instruction*, 28, 2, 1-15.

Thematic Organizer for the Sherlock Holmes Literature Passage
(The Adventure of the Dancing Men)

Both scientists and detectives are primarily concerned with the causes of events. Both scientists and detectives rely heavily on observation to gather evidence in their search for the truth, and both are concerned about the reliability or dependability of their observations. Detectives look for clues and investigate the events surrounding a case. Scientists use standard interviews and tests. Both gather evidence to increase the reliability of their observations.

Detectives and scientists also have hunches or hypotheses about the cause of the events. A hypothesis is an educated guess. During their investigations, detectives and scientists try to rule out hypotheses that are less than reasonable. For the detective the body of knowledge may include information about the chemical composition of cigar ashes. Detectives also make deductions about the behavior of people. For the scientist it may concern a description of the distribution of some disorder across different ages. But in each case, both detectives and scientists use prior knowledge to test their hunches or hypotheses.

Finally, both scientists and detectives tend to be extremely cautious about the conclusions they draw, and for similar reasons. Their conclusions must withstand critical scrutiny of a jury of critical peers or a court of law.

The comparison between detectives and scientists should not be carried too far. Detectives and scientists are different. One important difference is that a scientist is concerned with arriving at general statements that allow grouping apparently dissimilar events under a single rule or *generalization*. Detectives, on the other hand, wish to narrow their search to a single person or event. They use deduction to break down or narrow generalizations in solving their cases. They are less interested in the generalizations that might be produced from their work.

You will be asked to read two passages that concern the methods of *observation*, *hypotheses*, and *generalization* described above and be asked to answer the questions that follow.

In one of the passages you will read about a detective and his powers of *observation* and the way he formulates *hypotheses*. What do you think the detective will be concerned with? Write you answer here:

When you read this passage about the detective, find out if what you wrote agrees with what the detective does. You can read these pages again if you have any questions. You can look back at these pages as many times as you wish.

DIRECTIONS: Below are statements that relate to the reading. After each statement is a paragraph number which may help you make your decision. If you agree with the statement put a check mark in front of it. If you disagree with the statement leave it blank. One of the statements will ask you to write the paragraph numbers where the information can be found. You may look at the information on the front of this page and the reading passage as often as you wish. You can read these statements before and during your reading.

_____1. Sherlock Holmes uses the powers of observation and deduction in analyzing a person's behavior. (paragraphs 1-27).

_____ 2. There is evidence to indicate that Sherlock Holmes used the scientific method in some of his cases. (paragraphs 1, 12, and 16).

_____3. A complicated problem can be reduced to a simple solution once it has been broken down and explained. (paragraphs 10-16).

_____4. Paragraph 14 is an example of making generalizations rather than observations.

_____5. The stick men were obviously drawn by a child. (paragraphs 17, 18, 22, 23, 24, 25, 26. 27).

_____6. Write the *specific* paragraph numbers that show where Sherlock Holmes is using problem solving skills. Put a comma. (,) after each paragraph number.

Appendix B

Several studies have been conducted using thematic organizers with different populations. To prepare a thematic organizer the instructions are given below:

Developing a Thematic Organizer

The teacher:

1. Estimates the nature and degree of conceptual difficulty presented by the prose or narrative of the reading.

2. Identifies the theme of the passage. This theme is generally implied by the author, and therefore has not been explicitly defined.

3. Writes a paragraph(s) which introduces the theme called a thematic concept to be studied. Sets the scene by introducing the thematic concept in a setting believed to be relevant to the students' experiences.

4. Writes a paragraph(s), which either clarifies or elaborates upon the thematic concept. The paragraph(s) should define the thematic concept and present an analogy between the ideas in the text and the experiences of the students. Ideas within this paragraph(s) can be linked to relevant Internet sites that provide additional information for the student to read, view, and/or listen.

5. Composes each paragraph of the thematic organizer to contain a topic sentence followed by sentences with supporting details. These sentences should be written using explicit connectives, words that relate ideas in one sentence to the ideas to another sentence.

    Examples of explicit connectives are:

    1. *Reference* (e.g., These poor people could not own their own land. *They* did not have much money for food or houses.)
    2. *Conjunction* (e.g., The reformers were *also* called muckrakers.)
    3. *Lexical* (e.g., The reformers tried to help people. *These reformers* wanted everyone to have a fair chance to make a living.)

6. Asks students to make a prediction statement either orally or written concerning what they anticipate they will be reading. If written, students can note their thoughts and feelings in a journal, electronic notebook, or e-mail note for the teacher to respond.

7. Constructs statements that describe the thematic concept. At the end of each statement, paragraph number(s) are provided where the students can refer to make decisions concerning its relevance or irrelevance. Some statements may be linked to relevant Internet sites. The students are to place a check mark beside the statement to which they agree or to leave it blank if they disagree.

2 + 2 ≠ 4 ?

> Thus is man that great and true *Amphibium* whose nature is disposed
> to live not only like other creatures in diverse elements, but in divided
> and distinguished worlds.
>
> — Thomas Browne, *Religio Medici* (1642)

When is equal unequal? When the *uncertainty* within an equation is not explained. The composite Sherlock Holmes resides not in one but divided into two distinguished worlds: the visible and the invisible. He crosses both worlds to resolve uncertainties.

Monsignor Ronald A. Knox closes his treatise, "You know my methods, Watson: apply them."[72] The statement seems to imply a simplistic adding of parts to obtain the whole; just as is the equation 2 + 2 = 4. Not apparent is the way that Sherlock Holmes *applies* his methods to derive answers that is markedly different from that of Watson. A method that is not straight forward or tidy, and that involves a mix of elements and an answer that is more than a simple sum. His process and outcome is displayed as Sherlock Holmes perceives the event, applies both forward and inverse reasoning and uses his imagination to interpret an event. Yet, much of his thinking is complex and not easily revealed.

In the logical world of Scotland Yard detectives, for example, two plus two must equal four. However, in the world of Sherlock Holmes the events both logical and empirical may still add up to four, but be unequal.[73] When reading a Sherlock Holmes story we may encounter unusual story elements that disrupt the story's structure and use of our prior knowledge, making the events incongruent within our intuitive theories. These differences may intrude upon our individual problem solving impeding our solutions in favor of waiting for them to be resolved by Sherlock Holmes. Likewise, Scotland Yard detectives are stymied when applying generic practices to similar crimes. They become deterred by incongruities, and once confused seek advice from Sherlock Holmes in hopes of finding a resolution. Holmes listens, processes the events, and then

---

[72]Monsignor Ronald Arbuthnot Knox, "Studies in the Literature of Sherlock Holmes." This paper was first presented at the Bodley Club, Merton College, 10 March 1911, published in *The Blue Book Magazine* in 1912 and again later in *Essays in Satire* in 1928. See http://www.diogenes-club.com/knox.htm

[73] Sherlock Holmes ponders this dilemma when weighing his instincts and the value of his theory when they go against the facts of the police and the intellectual capability of a jury, *The Adventure of the Norwood Builder*.

enters a world where the logical and the empirical reside. It is within this world that events are classified, questions reformulated, and new information is gathered.

Monsignor Knox's message is direct implying methods that are observable and easily replicated; however, the irony of Sherlock's reasoning processes demand unconventional thinking. Even though Watson is familiar with Holmes' methods he has difficulty applying them. Watson has seen Holmes acting on the events of his cases and explaining his solution; yet he does not "apply" problem solving methods to satisfy Holmes. But can Watson be blamed for such faulty problem solving when Sherlock Holmes provides contradicting statements? "You know my method. It is founded upon the observance of trifles" (*The Boscombe Valley Mystery*). Then, "I have no time for trifles" (*A Study in Scarlet*). Then again, "It is, of course, a trifle, but there is nothing so important as trifles" (*The Man with the Twisted Lip*). What complicates these statements is the use of specific determiners as absolutes: "no" and "nothing." When Watson tries to use Holmes' methods, his efforts are criticized and it is Holmes who demeans Watson's ability to draw inferences (*The Adventure of the Blue Carbuncle*).

Perhaps a more likely explanation for Watson's lack of application, are the kinds of thought processes invoked by Sherlock Holmes that differ from those of Watson, just as they do from Lestrade and the other Scotland Yarders, perhaps even from ours. It is not the trifles (the facts), but the way in which the "facts" are viewed and interpreted. *Facts are not truths* and the reality of their value as a record of an event is dependent upon the relevant connection to the event itself. Coleridge remarked that facts are "in the nature and parts of premises."[74] Distinguishing among facts and assessing their worth display Sherlock Holmes' highest form of the art of detection (*The Reigate Squires*). For Watson and the police detectives, this type of scrutiny is often either overlooked or misused.

When confronted with a problem, Holmes assesses conditional probabilities and reasons through them by altering and reorganizing patterns of meaning as new information is available and synthesized. It is during these meditations that he evaluates the well-worn paths taken by the police and enters into a higher-order plane of reasoning that often places him into the mind-set of the perpetrator. And ironically, even though Holmes belittles C. Auguste Dupin, and Monsieur Lecoq, he uses their various ploys in his cases by reinterpreting the events and invoking a singular trait:

---

[74] Cited in M.H. Abrams, *The Mirror and the Lamp* (London: Oxford University Press, 1953). Original source, Coleridge, *Table Talk* (Oxford, 1917), 165; 27, Dec.1831.

"imagination."[75] Facts, coupled with visual acuity, give rise to ideas that spur his imagination. Holmes relies on his imagination to filter the facts, "I imagined what might have happened, acted upon the supposition, and find myself justified."[76] It is his ability to reconstitute the events by analyzing, discarding, synthesizing, and reorganizing information *and* then imagining how this mosaic can be interpreted and made visible that distinguishes Holmes from his rivals.

Like Watson, we as readers often have difficulty mapping the methods of inverse reasoning advocated by Holmes. Unlike Watson, we are not privy to Holmes' world, consumed with both the criminal and surreptitious reality. Unlike Watson, we do not have a physical presence at the scene, nor do we have the benefit of questioning Holmes about his paths of inquiry, especially those paths that differ from the conventional. Our recourse is to trace the line of inquiry offered by the narrative in hopes of reconciling the facts with our theory. This involves recognizing similarities and differences, evaluating, and interpreting meanings, values, and truths in keeping with reality. This reality is situated within the world of 1895, embedded within the political, social, cultural, and historical milieu of our understanding. The experiences encountered by Sherlock Holmes place us into a labyrinth of mental guesses that are clarified once they are understood by our own rewriting of the narrative.

It is within the realm of "backward reasoning" that distinguishes both Holmes and Dupin. Holmes notes, in *A Study in Scarlet*, that few use this cognitive process; however, it was described by the Rev. Thomas Bayes in 1643 an English mathematician and Presbyterian minister and later by Charles Sanders Peirce in 1903 an American philosopher, mathematician, and scientist.[77] Bayes theorem is predicated on decision analysis from which the introduction of new information is used to adjust the probabilities. As new information is gathered and processed the degree to which our beliefs are revised in an inverse manner is determined by the soundness of newly found data. In essence, backward mapping is the process of dealing with *uncertainty* and assigning probabilities to events that might happen. Joseph Kadane revisited backward reasoning by relating it to Bayes Theorem as it applies mathematically to the kind of

---

[75] In *A Study in Scarlet* examples are given of Sherlock Holmes imagining events before they are revealed. Also this trait is exhibited in *The Hound of the Baskervilles, Silver Blaze,* and *The Adventure of the Musgrave Ritual.*
[76] *Silver Blaze.*
[77] Thomas Bayes, "An Essay Toward Solving a Problem in the Doctrine of Chances," *Philosophical Transactions of the Royal Society,* 1763. Published posthumously. See also http://www.stat.ucla.edu/history/essay.pdf. Charles Sanders Peirce, *Collected Papers. (CP). Band I-VI. (Hrsg.) Charles Hartshorne und Paul Weiß. (Harvard University Press 1931-1935. Band VII, VIII. (Hrsg.) Arthur W. Burks. 1958).*

reasoning used by both Sherlock Holmes and M. Dupin.[78] He concludes that both Doyle's Holmes and Poe's Dupin use the principles of this theory in their thought patterns when dealing with uncertainty and exercise probability when calculating their resolutions.

Two cases, and their respective events, that exemplify this Bayesian theory of inverse reasoning are Poe's *The Purloined Letter* and Doyle's *The Final Problem*. In *The Purloined Letter*, M. Dupin mirrors the thought processes of Minister D. by situating himself within the reasoning that leads to his recovering the incriminating letter (see Appendix A, story map). *The Final Problem* is a parallel story in which Holmes puts himself within the mind of Professor Moriarty as he plans his deceptive journey from his mortal enemy. He couches his plan by imagining the events he perceives will be followed by Moriarty (see Appendix B, story map).

Putting two and two together is more often than not problematic puzzles for the police. Their answers may or may not add to four:

$$2 + 2 \neq 4 ?$$

"You mean two plus two is less than four? How can that be?
OK, you want me to pour two ounces of water into this measuring cup and then pour two ounces of alcohol into the same measuring cup. Wait a minute! Why doesn't the liquid rise to four ounces?

 You mean that when the two different kinds of liquids are combined into one measuring cup that it is less than four? In this case, two plus two is not four? Why does this happen? You say because the molecules that make up water and those that make up alcohol are shaped in such a fashion that when they are combined they are able to fit closer together and therefore take up less volume than when they are separate?

So, you say a *counting event* and a *chemical event* are different events? Yeah? Arithmetic deals with numbers. Chemistry deals with factual events of chemical behavior. Oh. Now I see: The *logical* and the *empirical* are two different events. Not the same kind of event."[79]

---

[78] See Joseph B. Kadane, "Bayesian Thought in Early Modern Detective Stories: Monsieur Lecoq, C. Auguste Dupin and Sherlock Holmes," *Statistical Science*, vol. 24, no. 2, 2009, 238-243.
[79] D. Bob Gowin and Marino C. Alvarez, *The Art of Educating with V Diagrams* (New York and Cambridge UK: Cambridge University Press, 2005), 8-9.

This unexpected result, once demonstrated, clarifies the uncertainty and enables the reader to grasp the meaning with two kinds of educative events. Holmes and Dupin do the same when they recombine and reformulate data during their reasoning while making disparate events equal and meaningful. The wake of this reasoning, like a conjuror, is based on revealing both facts and the events surrounding the facts. For Holmes it is this invisibility of his thinking serving as a cloak of uncertainty that separates the ordinary person from those more reasoned.[80]

When the inspectors from Scotland Yard consult with Sherlock Holmes it is because the events that they have undertaken do not add up in ways that help them solve a case. They confuse the event with the kind of thought processing required to understand the event. Sherlock Holmes listens to their explanation of the events and then uses the principle of Bayes theorem of inverse probabilities by categorizing the events and working towards a solution. He uses his imagination and sense of reasoning to simplify complexity. The irony of simplifying complexity for Holmes more often than not involves Watson. For Holmes simplifying complexity demands that *meaning* must be first grasped and then shared in order to formulate connection-making among complex ideas and events. And the value of Watson during this reasoning process cannot be underestimated as a loyal and trusted confidant. The world of Sherlock Holmes is divided into logical and empirical, and although he may reach a resolution that seems, like the example equation, to be unequal, the reasoning processes once revealed are made visible and understandable to the reader.

---

[80] Holmes separates himself from an "ordinary" person when deciding "when" and "how" to explain his reasoning. *The Crooked Man* and *A Study in Scarlet.*

Appendix A*

The Purloined Letter

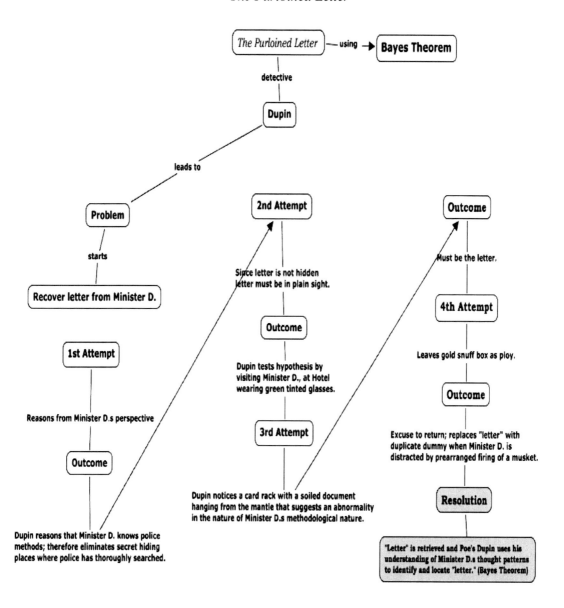

The Purloined Letter — using → **Bayes Theorem**

detective

Dupin

leads to

Problem

starts

Recover letter from Minister D.

1st Attempt

Reasons from Minister D.s perspective

Outcome

Dupin reasons that Minister D. knows police methods; therefore eliminates secret hiding places where police has thoroughly searched.

2nd Attempt

Since letter is not hidden letter must be in plain sight.

Outcome

Dupin tests hypothesis by visiting Minister D., at Hotel wearing green tinted glasses.

3rd Attempt

Dupin notices a card rack with a soiled document hanging from the mantle that suggests an abnormality in the nature of Minister D.s methodological nature.

Outcome

Must be the letter.

4th Attempt

Leaves gold snuff box as ploy.

Outcome

Excuse to return; replaces "letter" with duplicate dummy when Minister D. is distracted by prearranged firing of a musket.

Resolution

"Letter" is retrieved and Poe's Dupin uses his understanding of Minister D.s thought patterns to identify and locate "letter." (Bayes Theorem)

*NOTE: The events show the "backward reasoning" process by M. Dupin using Bayes Theorem and is capsulated in the Resolution that is shaded.

Appendix B*

The Final Problem

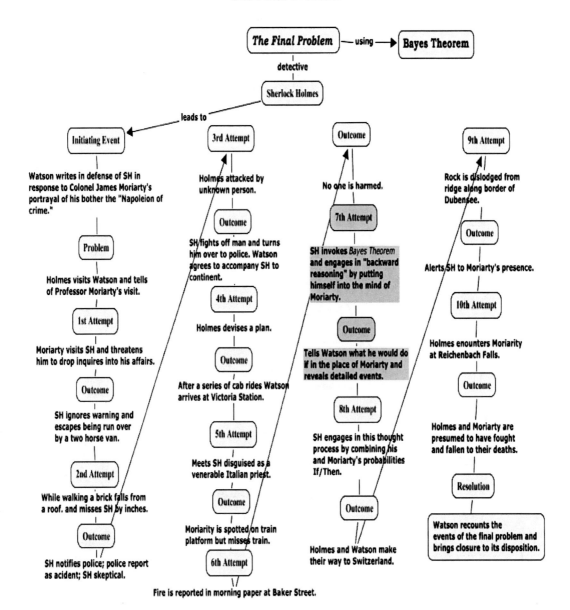

*NOTE: Attempt 7 and Outcome are shaded to show how Sherlock Holmes uses Bayes Theory in this story.

68

The Valley of Fear: Three Missing Words[81]

It's a simple statement: "Captain Marvin is my name – of the Coal and Iron" [Police]," yet it has a profound association with the events of the story, *The Valley of Fear*. The historical context of which is political and social, and of suspect constitutionality.

Conspicuously missing from the writings of Part Two, *The Valley of Fear*, the American edition, are the words "coal and iron."[82] David Randall, in *BSJ's* first volume (1946), suggested further examination of the omission of these three words in the story.[83] After searching *BSJ* articles; reviewing the articles edited by Steven T. Doyle; reading annotations by William S. Baring-Gould and also Leslie S. Klinger; and, examining books by Alistair Duncan and also Joseph Green and Peter Ridgway Watt, I learned that this issue is still not addressed.[84] This essay draws on some possible reasons for this deletion in the American edition, in which the publisher substituted a more neutral word "mine" for "coal and iron."

I propose that striking the three words and substituting "mine" was more than a simple exchange of words. The effect was to portray the "mine" police as a peace-keeping force rather than a regulatory power under the control of colliery operators. A second premise that I propose for this change relates to the popularity of A. Conan Doyle

---

[81]A version of this essay appeared as Marino C. Alvarez. "The Valley of Fear: Three Missing Words." *Baker Street Journal*. 61, no. 2, (Summer, 2011): 33-37. Reprinted with the kind permission of *The Baker Street Journal*.

[82] These words do not appear in *The Complete Sherlock Holmes*, by Arthur Conan Doyle, Doubleday and Company, Garden City, New York, 1920. They do appear in the Heritage Press publication edited by Edgar W. Smith, Sir Arthur Conan Doyle *The Final Adventures of Sherlock Holmes*, Heritage Press, New York 1952. (In this book *The Valley of Fear* is reproduced from the version first published in 1915 by George H. Doran, New York).

[83] David A. Randall, "The Valley of Fear Bibliographically Considered," *Baker Street Journal*. Vol. 1, No. 2 (April 1946): 232-237.

[84] Stephen T. Doyle (editor). *Murderland: A Companion Volume to The Baker Street Irregulars' Expedition to The Valley of Fear* (New York: The Baker Street Irregulars, 2004); William Baring-Gould, *The Annotated Sherlock Holmes* (New York: Clarkson N. Potter Publisher), 1967; Leslie S. Klinger, *The Valley of Fear by Arthur Conan Doyle. Edited, with Annotations*. The Sherlock Holmes Reference Library (Indianapolis, IN: Gasogene Books, 2005); Alistair Duncan, *Eliminate the Impossible: An Examination of the World of Sherlock Holmes on Page and Scree*n (London, UK: MX Publishing, 2008); Joseph Green & Peter Ridgway Watt. Alas, *Poor Sherlock: The Imperfections of the World's Greatest Detective (to say nothing of his medical friend* (Kent England: Chancery House Press, 2007).

and Sherlock Holmes in the United States. These writings were influential in capturing the imagination and hearts of the American public and furthering the appeal of Doyle himself and the Sherlock Holmes stories, in particular. Thus, it was important to distance Doyle and Holmes from the unpopularity of the "coal and iron" police.

Randall reasons that altering the English edition by striking "German" and inserting "Swedish" as Shafters' nationality was due to the emotions of the British public during World War I, and that the American editor changing the *Ancient Order of Freemen* from the English version to the *Eminent Order of Freemen* had a specific purpose. This latter change Randall speculates occurred "with a view to placating the Irish vote." He likely felt that the book's influence would in some way affect the voting interests of Irish-Americans. The association of "Ancient Order" with "Coal and Iron" Police would have provoked not only Irish-Americans but also other Americans regardless of nationality or ethnic group. Randall's question concerning the changing of the three words "coal and iron" requires further inspection.

The Valley of Fear provides an historical context for the events that transpired in Pennsylvania. It parallels an actual incident that occurred in which equivocal opinions surround its circumstances involving a socioeconomic struggle between the laborer and the employer. I propose that there is evidence to suggest that the deletion of the "coal and iron" police in the American edition may have been to stem further incitement among miners and labors and the American public about this private police agency. The fact that the Coal and Iron police were beyond the boundaries of the public law was the indirect result of the state legislature passing the 1905 law establishing the organization of the State Constabulary to oversee this private force.

The Coal and Iron Police was created by State Act 228 passed in 1865 by the Pennsylvania State Legislature initially for railroads to organize private police forces. The following year a supplement to this Act authorized that it be expanded to "embrace all corporations, firms, or individuals, owning, leasing, or being in possession of any colliery, furnace, or rolling mill with this commonwealth."[85] The Coal and Iron Police was a private force employed to enforce and protect colliery interests.[86] Many of their

---

[85] See Coal and Iron Police, Pennsylvania General Assembly, Statutes (February 27, 1885), no. 228 and (April 11, 1866), supplement no. 87. Retrieved August 14, 2009 from http://www.mcintyrepa.com/coalandironpolice.htm

[86] The Coal and Iron Police protected the mine owners property and personal safety. Franklin P. Gowen hired this force for protection. Likewise the Crawshay and Bailey families built a fortress to protect themselves from mine workers in 1816 for fear of a workers revolt. See website by Jeffrey L. Thomas. Photographs of the tower and its description: Nantyglo Round Towers. Nantyglo Wales. http://www.thomasgenweb.com/nantyglo_round_towers.html

methods were intimidating, illegal, and forcibly imposed on mine workers, union representatives, and local residents. Pennsylvania Governor Samuel W. Pennypacker initiated the establishment of the Pennsylvania State Constabulary in 1906, in part, to monitor the Coal and Iron Police's practices which he regarded as unconstitutional in their enforcement of mine workers and strike breakers.[87] However, since a requirement stated that a member must be unmarried to join the State Constabulary, those that did marry after being on the force often became part of the Coal and Iron Police. It was widely reported that state police and the coal and iron police were joined in efforts to quell civil liberties of those whom they perceived as either causing a disturbance or were perceived as potential disrupters.[88] It is plausible to assume that there was collusion among these two agencies, along with the Pinkerton's, protecting company interests.

Cleveland Moffett reports incidents of the intimidating practices imposed on the mine superintendents by the order in this story's locale. However, these accounts are taken from the "Archives of The Pinkerton Detective Agency" and may have been biased.[89] Yet, there is evidence to suggest that some superintendents in charge of mining operations sometimes took unfair advantage over the mine workers verging on discrimination and civil rights violations, and subscribing to dictatorial practices. Denise Weber, for example, describes Otto Hoffman superintendent of the Vinton Colliery Company, the equivalent of a "feudal lord" referred to as "Pappy" or "King Otto" who monitored not only mine operations but the daily activities of the workers including the imposition of unlawful voting practices. Citing Hoffman's diary entries she states that he sanctioned and encouraged the "tipping of the hat" by foreign employees and referred to these immigrants as "Payday Hunks." Miners were required to buy groceries, clothing,

---

[87] See Pennsylvania Historical & Museum Collection. Retrieved September 5, 2009 from http://www.portal.state.pa.us/portal/server.pt/community/1879-1951/4284/samuel_whitaker_pennypacker/469087
Interestingly, Governor Samuel W. Pennypacker of Pennsylvania consulted with the British government and conceived the State Constabulary that was modeled after the British Constabulary of Ireland. They were mounted horseman carrying a .38 caliber pistol, a hickory baton, and wore bobby-style helmets. See Stephen H. Norwood, *Strikebreaking and Intimidation: Mercenaries and Masculinity in Twentieth-Century America*, (Chapel Hill: University of North Carolina Press), 2002; also Explore PA History, http://explorepahistory.com/hmarker.php?markerId=940

[88] Norwood, 124.

[89] Cleveland Moffett, "The Overthrow of the Molly Maguires," in Stephen T. Doyle, editor, *Murderland: A Companion Volume to The Baker Street Irregulars' Expedition to The Valley of Fear* (New York: The Baker Street Irregulars, 2004). Within this same *McClures Magazine*, Vol. IV, (December, 1894-May 1895), New York & London: S.S. McClure, Moffett published three other articles all from the Archives of the Pinkerton Detective Agency: "The Rock Island Express Robbery," "The Destruction of the Reno Gang." and "The Pollack Diamond Robbery."

and household goods at the company store and the failure to do so resulted in dismissal. During times of strikes or labor unrest, the company police stood outside the privately owned stores preventing customers (workers and out-of-towners) from entering.[90] An unconfirmed report stated that the Coal and Iron Police would come to the home of a miner, put a sandwich in a lunch bucket and forcibly take the man to the mine if he failed to appear during his work schedule.[91] The Coal and Iron Police also engaged in evicting disruptive mine workers and their families from their homes and were accused of rape, kidnapping, assault, and murder.[92]

Although the story appears in 1914-1915, the events portrayed took place in the 1870s following the Civil War. The social and working conditions that existed then continued through the 1920s in regions of Pennsylvania, together with the ongoing diligence exercised by the Coal and Iron Police. This is an important point since at the time of publication of *The Valley of Fear* in the United States, the plight of the miner and laborer, and the writings of muckrakers advocating a need for social justice were vivid among the populace.[93]

A second reason for this omission is the popularity of Arthur Conan Doyle and Sherlock Holmes in the United States. Conan Doyle had completed a successful lecture tour in New York, Princeton, and Pennsylvania in 1894-1895. Major James Pond had promoted and scheduled talks and readings in thirty cities. Sherlock Holmes was the object of audience interest. Then a year before publication of *The Valley of Fear* in America, Conan Doyle returned to New York City in May 1914. It is possible that he met with his American editor and discussed the events associated with the coal and iron police.[94] The popularity of the Sherlock Holmes stories in America during this period

---

[90] Denise Dusza Weber, *Delano's Domain: A History of Warren Delano's Mining Towns of Vintondale, Wehrum and Claghorn, Volume 1, 1789-1930* (Indiana, PA: A.G. Halldin Publishing Company, Inc., 1991.

[91] See article by Nancy Moses, Food for Thought: Franklin B. Gowen's Ceremonial Bowl. Reprinted from the Pennsylvania Historical Society archives. Retrieved August 15, 2009. http://www.freewebs.com/wigganspatch/franklingowen.htm.

[92] See Coal and Iron Police. Retrieved August 14, 2009 from http://www.mcintyrepa.com/coalandironpolice.htm

[93] See Richard P. Mulcahy, University of Pittsburgh at Titusville, "An Essay from 19th Century U.S. Newspapers Database Mining and Extraction." Retrieved September 5. 2009 from http://www.gale.cengage.com/DigitalCollections/whitepapers/9_GML33607_Mining_whtppr.pdf

[94] It may be a reasonable assumption since we know that Conan Doyle was friends with American editors such as Samuel McClure. He provided stories to his magazine and contributed financially to keep the magazine in production. See Andrew Lycett, *The Life and Times of Sir Arthur Conan*

may have influenced an editor's decision (even in consultation with Doyle) to modify the wording in anticipation of the ramifications associating "coal and iron" police depicted in the story. The tactics imposed by the Coal and Iron Police on the miners, residents, and out-of-town visitors may have resulted in the reading public becoming outraged by the reminder of these violations of civil and constitutional rights.

Holmes' popularity was at a high pitch with U.S. readership. When Sherlock Holmes is killed in *The Final Problem*, the *Strand* lost 20,000 subscribers, with letters expressing outrage. In New York, "Keep Holmes Alive" societies came into being. William Gillette's portrayal of Sherlock Holmes at the Garrick Theater in New York City on November 6, 1899 lasted for 230 performances and resulted in more than 1,300 performances overall.

With the publication of *The Hound of the Baskervilles* in America, 50,000 copies were sold in the United Stated edition the first day it appeared. In 1903, both the *Strand* in August 1901and *Collier's Weekly* advertised the return of Sherlock Holmes and spurred Sherlockian interest to the joy of readers in England and America. In *The Adventure of the Noble Bachelor*, Doyle extends an alliance with American readers when Holmes hopes for a union between the United States and United Kingdom whereby being "citizens of the same world-wide country under a flag which shall be a quartering of the Union Jack with the Stars and Stripes." Doyle's popularity is enhanced further with his direct involvement solving real-life cases; instrumental in the acquittals of George Edaljis and Oscar Slater.[95]

Philosophy combines with prophesy when Sherlock Holmes, speaking to Inspector MacDonald says, "The old wheel turns and the same spoke comes up. It has all been done before, and will be again." In real life Pinkerton Detective James McParland, the undercover chief witness for the prosecution, and portrayed in the story as Birdy Edwards/Jack Douglas is like the spoke in a wheel. He again reappears in a case involving the Western Miners Federation (1906-1907) in Idaho as the chief witness for the prosecution. However, McParland is found guilty of perjury. Clarence Darrow, who had defended the trade union leaders in this case, drew a comparison between the Molly

---

Doyle (New York: Free Press, 2007); Also, Ray E. Boomhower retrieved September 14, 2009 from http://www.depauw.edu/library/archives/ijhof/inductees/mcclure.htm
[95] Conan Doyle wrote a series of articles for the *Daily Telegraph* about the Edalji case. It is important to note that partially as a result of this case the Court of Criminal Appeal was established in 1907. See http://www.siracd.com/life_case1.shtml; In 1912 Conan Doyle published *The Case of Oscar Slater* that examined evidence at the trial that was not introduced. See http://www.siracd.com/life/life_case2.shtml

Maguire case and this one in which he cast doubt upon the integrity of McParland.[96] One wonders if the circumstances of this case may have entered the mind of the American editor and led to real-life questions surrounding the integrity of Edwards/Douglas and his exploits in the story.

Combining these two assertions, one a feared association with overzealous tactics by some members of the Coal and Iron Police; and, two a concern about the impact on the popularity of A. Conan Doyle and Sherlock Holmes in America may have been the impetus behind the use of a blue pencil to line out the three words by the American editor. If the American editor invoked the technique that Sherlock Holmes uses in his cases; that of backward reasoning, it is likely that his decision was made based on these past circumstances that surrounded this event at the time of publication and the consequences that may have arisen.[97] On June 30, 1934, Governor Gifford Pinchot used his own blue pencil and revoked all coal and iron police commissions in the State of Pennsylvania.

---

[96] See Seamus Metress, *The Molly Maguires and the Early Struggle of Labor*. Retrieved September 1, 2009 from http://www.irishfreedom.net/Cultural/Articles/The%20Molly%20Maguires.htm
[97] In *A Study of Scarlet*, Holmes tells Watson that, "In solving a problem... the grand thing is to be able to reason backwards....There are fifty who can reason synthetically for one who can reason analytically."

The Stock-Broker's Clerk: Parallels and Parodies

> After all, it is a question of money with these fellows, and I
> have the British Treasury behind me. If it's on the market
> I'll buy it - if it means another penny on the income tax.
> It is conceivable that the fellow might hold it back to see what
> bids come from this side before he tries his luck on the other.

(*The Adventure of the Second Stain*)

The canon is replete with incidents that repeat character traits, plot structures, and story resolutions that are similar in nature lending themselves to parallel events and parodies of comedic circumstances. Such is the case of *The Stock-Brokers Clerk* as it parallels the events depicted in *The Red-Headed League* and *The Adventure of the Three Garridebs*.[98] This essay addresses several parallels and includes some parodies using *The Stock-Broker's Clerk* as its core with strands linking to *The Red-Headed* League and *The Adventure of the Three Garridebs* as they relate to clients and their antagonists.

Synopsis - The Stock-Broker's Clerk

Sherlock Holmes is visited by Hall Pycroft who is somewhat perplexed at the events that have transpired over the course of a week. First, he is unemployed whereupon he receives a letter of acceptance from the Mawson & Williams brokerage firm hiring him without ever meeting him. Next, he is visited at his flat by Arthur Pinner, a financial agent, and offered the position of a business manager at Franco-Midland Hardware Company, which he has never heard of and to which he is to leave immediately for another city, Birmingham, without any notice to Mawson & Williams. Upon arrival he is met by a person whom he believes to be Arthur's brother, Harry, but in reality is Arthur himself no longer disguised wearing a beard and dark hair, but is now clean-shaven with light hair. He is taken to depressed office surroundings and dismayed at the lack of office features and sparse furniture. His first task is to copy the names of hardware firms from a Paris directory list. After a week of continuous activity, he begins to question its value while noticing that both Arthur and Harry have a gold tooth in the same location thereby surmising that this is indeed the same man. After listening to his story Holmes takes Pycroft with him and visits Dr. Watson.

---

[98] Publication dates: *The Red-Headed League, The Strand Magazine,* August 1891 ; *The Stock-Broker's Clerk, The Strand Magazine,* March 1893 ; *The Adventure of the Three Garridebs, Collier's,* October 1924

Holmes, Watson, and Pycroft go to Birmingham to meet with Arthur/Harry Pinner. As they approach the office they see Pinner buying a newspaper and scurrying to the office. Upon entry, they find Pinner in an agitated state. He excuses himself, goes to another room where he attempts to hang himself. He is saved when Holmes and Watson break down the door and free him from hanging by his braces. The newspaper reports that Arthur/Harry's brother, Beddington #2 has replaced Pycroft at Mawson & Williams, murdered a man in an attempt to rob a "hundred thousand pounds worth of American railway bonds with a large amount of scrip in mines and other companies" and that he is under arrest.

Before leaving this summary it would be remiss if the circumstances that prompted Sherlock Holmes to visit Watson are not examined. For this event is interesting in and of itself. Watson has been married to Mary Morstan for three months. Likewise, he has bought and worked at a practice for the same period of time.[99] First Holmes visits Watson, second, Watson has bought a declining practice, and third, to no one's surprise he is ready at a moment's notice to bid his wife good-bye, write a note to his neighbor, also a physician who owes him a debt, and fourth, go with Holmes to Birmingham. But wait! Let's delve into this instance further. Why does Holmes visit Watson? Is Mary Morstan somewhat concerned that her newly-wed husband is leaving on impulse to accompany Holmes out of the city on a non-threatening excursion? What about Watson's financial prowess? Watson takes over a practice in financial demise. Remember he didn't have a practice before this one. Under Dr. Farquhar the practice declined from twelve hundred to a little more than three hundred pounds year. Does this seem to be a shrewd buy? Or does Watson expect a run on neighborhood illnesses? What about his neighbor who is in his "debt"? How often does he travel? Do any of these two practices sound as if they are overrun with patients?

What's with Holmes? As they depart, Holmes notices the brass plate and tells Watson that his neighbor is a physician. Watson just told him minutes earlier that he was leaving a note for his neighbor who was a doctor. Holmes then comments that Watson's practice is doing very well in comparison to his neighbor since his steps are worn 3 inches deeper. Never mind that these depressions have been in the making for 17 years and Watson has only lived on these premises three months. What Holmes fails to mention is that both steps are equally less worn since each had recently purchased their respective practices. As I read this section I paused and reflected on these circumstances. I wondered where this idea of two doctors with limited patients had its origin. And then,

---

[99] Alistair Duncan, *Eliminate the Impossible*. (Stanstead Abotts, Hertfordshire: MX Publishing, 2008).

it came to me. I envisioned these two houses next door to each other. I foresaw a third house in Southsea, Portsmouth, with smooth steps – not worn - and, peering through the window, another physician – an author – penning stories while waiting for his patients to appear at his practice. Then again, perhaps this observation is too farfetched.

In the Discussion section I revisit this instance of peculiarity regarding why Sherlock Holmes visits Watson.

Intervening Parallels and Parodies

There are parallels and parodies that emanate from *The Stock Brokers Clerk* that can be related to *The Red-Headed League* and *The Adventure of the Three Garridebs*. Several of these characteristics are given as they relate to the clients and antagonists in these three stories.

The Clients

In both *The Stock Broker's Clerk* and *The Red-Headed League* the clients are clerks whose responsibilities are to copy from either the Paris directory or the *Encyclopedia Britannica*, and in each instance, the furniture is sparse. Each engage in parallel circumstances; Jabez Wilson (eight weeks) and Hall Pycroft (one week) must not leave the premises or locale and copy from a listing. Nathan Garrideb, a collector of specimens, geological and anatomical, and of coins, is asked to travel to Birmingham to meet the third Garrideb. Each of the three is somewhat greedy and dim-witted. Although both Jabez and Hall can be considered less than quick, Nathan is single-minded and driven more by his scientific pursuits. All three are duped into leaving their premises on a wild-goose chase.

Take Hall Pycroft as an example. He is unemployed from his clerkship at Coxon and Woodhouse despite glowing recommendations from his superior by the name of Parker. He is offered employment with Mawson & Williams without being interviewed. Before he can report to this firm, he is offered a position at Franco-Midland Company, and is given an interview by Arthur Pinner as to his knowledge of stocks. Arthur Pinner asks Hall Pycroft about the price of Ayrshires. Pycroft replies, "A hundred and six and a quarter to a hundred and five and seven—eighths." The bid is higher than the asking price[100] Nevertheless he is just the man Mawson & Williams and Franco-Midland are looking for. The motto for these two firms seem to be: "Buy high and sell low."

---

[100] Julian Wolfe. From the Editor's Commonplace Book, *Baker Street Journal*, vol. 12. 4. (December, 1962): 245.

O'Donnell opines that in *The Red-Headed League*, Jabez Wilson's salary of four pounds a week was "a liberal income in the Britain of 1887."[101] In this instance, Holmes became somewhat suspicious of the pay and task required of Jabez Wilson. She further makes an analogy to the work performed by Hall Pycroft in *The Stock Broker's Clerk* at a brokerage firm at 200 pounds per annum and offered a higher wage of 500 pounds by another. When Holmes asks Pycroft, "What qualities have you, my friend, which would make your services so valuable?" His reply is, "None" which immediately arouses Holmes' senses of something awry. Of course, Hall doesn't find these offerings as being incongruous.

The physical features and attire of the clients are always described. In *The Red-Headed* League Jabez Wilson is "portly, sloppy, obese, and pompous." His trousers are "baggy, coat not clean, and a waistcoat that is drab." He has a "frayed top-hat and a faded brown overcoat with a wrinkled velvet collar." Hall Pycroft, *The Stock-Broker's Clerk,* on the other hand, is "smart, well-built, has an honest face and a crisp, yellow moustache." He also has a top-hat but his is "shiny and a neat black suit." His face is "round and cheery." Nathan Garrideb, *The Adventure of the Three Garridebs*, is a "tall, round-backed person, bald, and about sixty-odd years of age. He wears large round spectacles and a small projecting goat's beard combined with his stooping attitude to give him an expression of peering curiosity." He is classified as being eccentric.

The Antagonists

The most interesting are the antagonists with their similar villainous skills and their abundance of aliases. We have the Beddington brothers in *The Stock Broker's Clerk*. Beddington #1 is a skilled self-impersonator. Beddington #2 is a forger and cracksman. John Clay (*The Red-Headed League*) shares Beddington #2's skills as a forger and thief, but we can add "smasher." John Clay has royal blood, and is the fourth smartest man in London. Let's see: Holmes, Moriarty, Colonel Moran, then John Clay…. W.E. Dudley asks, "Where's Watson?" [102] The most interesting is James Winter (*The Adventure of the Three Garridebs*), who is a "killer" but would like to be a forger if he can get his hands on the counterfeit printing press.

---

[101] Margaret G. O'Donnell, "A Study in the Economics of Sherlock Holmes," *Baker Street Journal*, vol. 34, no. 4, (December, 1984): 227-233.
[102] W.E. Dudley, Dr. Watson's Triple Play, *Baker Street Journal*, vol. 23, no. 1, (March, 1973): 22-27.

Arthur Beddington (*The Stock Broker's Clerk*) has an alias of Harry which is his brother's name. John Clay (*The Red-Headed League*) uses the name of Vincent Spaulding, as if it is necessary to use an alias to deceive Jabez Wilson. James Winter (*The Adventure of the Three Garridebs*) is to be commended for remembering who he is and under what circumstances and location. He is James Winter when in Chicago, alias of John Garrideb in London, alias Morecroft which is an alias for James Winter, and Killer (no first name) Evans also an alias for James Winter. When reading this story, I imagined "Killer from Chicago" as stocky, gravel voiced, arms like sledgehammers, and a face that could… well…. Kill. Instead, he is characterized as "chubby and rather childlike." Does this description strike you as a Killer from Chicago? Isn't Yogi Bear "chubby and rather childlike?"

Also of note are their clever disguises. Arthur Pinner wears a beard and has dark hair. He dupes Hall Pycroft by assuming the dual role of his brother, Harry, by either shaving or removing his beard and lightening his hair. However, Hall is quick and perceptive to notice, after a week, that both have a gold tooth thereby making a penetrating analogy that both Arthur and Harry are one of the same. Beards are really a smart disguise. Of course, Mary Sutherland, *A Case of Identity*, can't recognize her step father, James Windibank whom she lives with, when he appears as Hosmer Angel with his "whiskers," a "gentle voice" and "tinted glasses." This disguise is more impressive when we realize that this one man is the person to whom she is dating and is going to marry. How many of us were fooled when we watched George Reeves as Superman on TV? Clark Kent with glasses; Superman without. He was difficult to keep track of. I could tell the difference because he wore a tight suit with an "S" and a cape when he was Superman and a felt fedora and a gray suit and glasses when he was Clark Kent. It wasn't easy. I often wondered how no one noticed the many times he flew out the same window of *The Daily Planet*.

In both *The Stock Broker's Clerk* and *The Adventure of the Three Garridebs* there are American connections. In *The Stock Broker's Clerk* there is a reference that James Winter (Killer) is from Chicago, and the mention of Moorville, Kansas. In *The Red-Headed League*, Lebanon, Pennsylvania is given. Although these cities serve as backdrops in both stories, the action takes place in England.

The Revolver: A Curious Incident

In *The Adventure of the Three Garridebs*, Killer Evans draws a revolver and fires wounding Watson. In the two illustrations by Sidney Paget both Holmes and Watson are pointing their revolvers at Evans as he emerges from the cellar. How does he have time to draw his revolver from his breast and fire at Watson? Why does Holmes hit him on the head with the butt of his revolver instead of shooting him?

John Clay in *The Red-Headed League* emerges from below a tunnel up into the cellar vault with revolver in hand. "WHY?" Who did he expect to come in contact with? Holmes hits Clay on wrist with hunting crop. Where's his revolver? Where is his walking stick he took to the pawn shop? What's he doing with a hunting crop in a bank basement vault? Let's not get into *how* Holmes anticipates Mr. Merryweather is going to be upset of missing his "rubber" match or *why* Holmes brings a pack of cards to placate him. Nor the reasons Holmes or Watson are inept locksmiths since in both *The Stock Broker's Clerk* and *The Sign of the Four* they break down the door.

Discussion

Drawing parallels and parodies that accompany these events among *The Stock Brokers Clerk*, *The Red-Headed League*, and *The Adventure of the Three Garridebs*, together with the client and antagonist comparisons are interesting. They serve to show how these three stories are similar in plot, characterization, and resolution. The clients were somewhat similar in wit and awareness. The antagonists all had aliases, two of which could trace their past to America, and all had as their goal the procurement of illicit money. In each of the stories the value of the money progresses in substantial increments. In *The Stock Brokers Clerk*, a hundred thousand pounds. In *The Red-Headed League*, French gold of two thousand napoleons together with a reserve of bullion. In *The Adventure of the Three Garridebs* a counterfeit printing press the implications of which are – priceless.

Focusing on *The Stock-Broker's Clerk* raises specific questions. Do the events described by Pycroft warrant Sherlock Holmes visiting Dr. Watson and asking to accompany him to Birmingham? Was it that Holmes missed his company after he married Mary Morstan? Recall that when he returns from hiatus he persuades Watson to sell his practice and return to Baker Street. Only later does Watson discover that Dr. Verner, who made the purchase, was a distant relative of Holmes who financed this transaction.[103] Or was it that Holmes needed him to continue chronicling his exploits? Who else could he count on to write these cases if not Watson? [104] Who else could he impress with his powers of deduction if not Watson? Perhaps in this story we get a

---

[103] See *The Adventure of the Norwood Builder*.
[104] Again in *The Adventure of the Norwood Builder*, Holmes dissuades credit and instead mentions to Lestrade that his historian may sometime mention this escapade in his chronicles. Published in the *Strand Magazine*, 1903.

glimpse of him having to again mystify Watson by attempting to reveal these powers such as the slippers and the related events when he deduces that Watson has had a cold, or the brass plate on his neighbor's house, or the mention of the worn steps. Not so much that these were noteworthy explanations, but rather that they served to provide the reader with a more perceptive insight into Holmes' need for continued friendship.

While *The Stock-Broker's Clerk* may not be one of the better stories in the canon, it does serve to raise interesting questions that go beyond the events depicted in the story. It gives us a glimpse into Sherlock Holmes' life after Watson and his need to have Watson as a friend, chronicler, and companion.

Thumb-less in Eyford

"Crime is common. Logic is rare."

(*The Adventured of the Copper Beeches*)

   The Engineer's Thumb is the only story in the Canon in which Sherlock Holmes does virtually nothing, and as reported by Joseph Green and Peter Ridgway Watt, fails at the one opportunity he has to accomplish a resolution.[105] This story features Victor Hatherley as the teller of the tale and Watson as the scribe. The story focuses on this hydraulic engineer called to fix a hydraulic press and his exploits surrounding his visit to the house in the fictional town of Eyford, located in Berkshire near the borders of Oxfordshire, and within seven miles of Reading. A view of stations at Reading, circa 1865–70, with the South Eastern Railway's station on the left, and the Great Western Railway's station at the higher level on the right.[106]

---

[105]Joseph Green & Peter Ridgway Watt, *Alas, Poor Sherlock: The imperfections of the world's greatest detective (to say nothing of his medical friend* (Kent, England: Chancery House Press, 2007).
[106] Wikipedia Encyclopedia. Retrieved
http://en.wikipedia.org/wiki/Reading_Southern_railway_station October 17, 2011.

The map below provides a setting for the fictional Town of Eyford located within seven miles of Reading.[107]

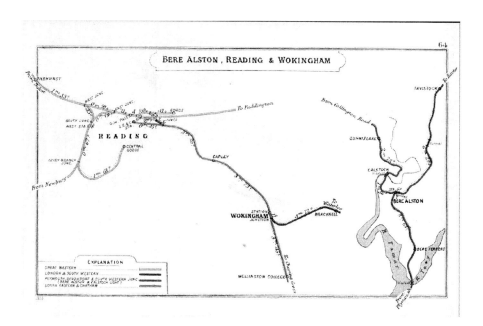

This essay describes the instances experienced by Victor Hatherley since he is the central figure of the story. The only visible sign that a crime has been committed is the thumb found on the window sill and the fact that Victor Hatherley is missing one. While the tale provides the reader with a series of events, these events are difficult to understand. For example, there are many unanswered questions that remain once the story is told: the roving cap; the thumb on the window-sill; a hydraulic press built on the second floor; the escape panel in the hydraulic press; the long-lasting house fire despite firemen and three fire engines on the scene; a police station three miles away and yet Hatherley travels to London; St. Mary's Hospital less than a hundred yards from Paddington Station yet he is guided to Dr. Watson's surgery; the ability of Victor Hatherley to withstand such an ordeal and still manages to return to Eyford.

This story map shows the events experienced by Victor Hatherley while in Eyford.

---

[107] Wikipedia Encyclopedia. Retrieved http://en.wikipedia.org/wiki/File:Bere_Alston,_Reading_%26_Wokingham_RJD_64.jpg, October 17, 2011.

What Happened to Victor in Eyford?

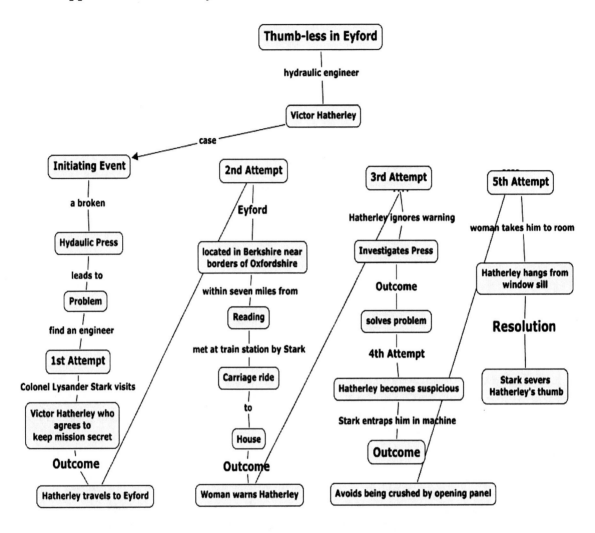

A hydraulic press serves as a potential death chamber for Victor Hatherley. The second floor press is composed of metal with a large iron trough. Baring-Gould refers to this machine as being one designed by Sir Charles Davy in 1886 and cites Ian McNeil for this insight.[108] The so-called coiners use inappropriate metals (nickel and tin), the

_____

[108] Ian McNeil, "An Engineer's Thoughts on 'The Engineer's Thumb. "*The Sherlock Holmes Journal.* Vol. V, No. 4 (Spring, 1962): 108-110. As cited in William Baring-Gould, William. *The Annotated Sherlock Holmes, vol. II.* (New York: Clarkson N. Potter, Inc., 1967), 213.

depicted butcher cleaver is unwieldy, and the location of the hydraulic press on the second floor with a stone floor is somewhat confounding.

Hatherley's Tale

He is approached by Colonel Lysander Stark to come on a mission of secrecy in which he must promise not to tell anyone either before or after his mission is completed. Given that Stark does not reveal the name of the person who recommended Hatherley, that Hatherley is an orphan and a bachelor residing alone in London, and has had only three consultations in two years earning a meager £ 27 10s, about $137.50 U.S. at the time, and wasn't aware that fuller's earth, could be found in more than two places in England one wonders who and what he could tell on such short notice if he was so inclined.[109] The question of the fuller's earth reveals Hatherley's need to increase his coffers.

> 'The only point which I could not quite understand was what use you could make of a hydraulic press in excavating fuller's-earth, which, as I understand, is dug out like gravel from a pit.'
>
> " 'Ah!' said he carelessly, 'we have our own process. We compress the earth into bricks, so as to remove them without revealing what they are.

Hatherley, although not aware that fuller's earth exists in more than two places in England, and skeptic about the use of a hydraulic press to be used to extract this substance from the ground is not fazed by being told that these persons have developed a special process to accomplish the task of making bricks "so as to remove them without revealing what they are." This discrepancy of his knowledge seems to be reconciled by the sum offered by Colonel Lysander Stark of fifty guineas, about $262.50 U.S., a sizable amount more than his two year income.[110] This fee prompts Victor Hatherley to go to Eyford to fix the malfunctioning hydraulic press.

A story map of the key events that happen to Victor Hatherley is shown below.

---

[109] William Baring-Gould. *The Annotated Sherlock Holmes, vol. II.* (New York: Clarkson N.Potter, Inc., 1967, p. 213.
[110] Barring-Gould, p. 218.

What a Day!

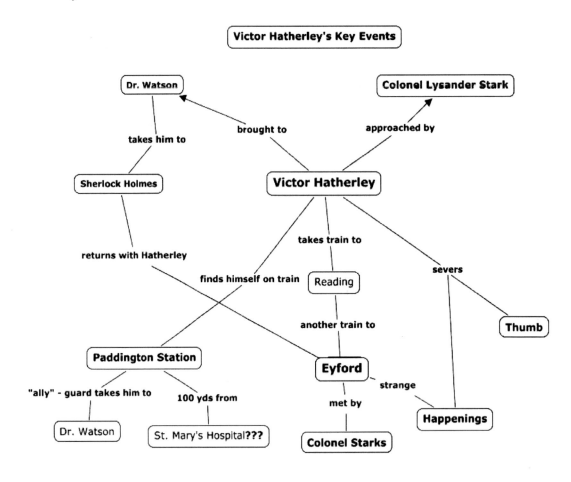

Victor Hatherley's Key Events

- Dr. Watson
- Colonel Lysander Stark
- Sherlock Holmes — takes him to Dr. Watson
- Victor Hatherley
  - brought to Dr. Watson
  - approached by Colonel Lysander Stark
  - takes train to Reading
  - finds himself on train
  - severs Thumb
- Sherlock Holmes — returns with Hatherley
- Reading — another train to Eyford
- Paddington Station
  - "ally" - guard takes him to Dr. Watson
  - 100 yds from St. Mary's Hospital???
- Eyford
  - met by Colonel Starks
  - strange Happenings

Understanding how one person can be subjected to so many traumatic experiences, outlined below, in a twenty-four hour period is astounding.

Victor's Timeline: The asterisk denotes the beginning of the time period given in the story.

A Summer Day in 1889

7:30 am -	Awakes, dresses, and eats breakfast.
8:30 am -	Leaves for work.
*9:00 am -	**Begins workday at Victoria Street.**
3:45 pm -	Visited by Colonel Lysander Stark.
4:00 pm -	Leaves office.
4:30 pm – 8::00 pm -	Eats dinner, packs, and leaves for Paddington Station.
8:30 pm –	Arrives at Paddington Station.
9:00 pm -10:00 pm -	Takes train to Reading.
10:00 pm -	Arrives at Reading.
10:40 pm -	Takes train to Eyford
11:15 pm -	Arrives at Eyford.
11:15 pm – 12:15am	One hour carriage ride to house.
12:15 am – 1:30 am	Meets, Mr. Ferguson (Dr. Becher) and Elise; leaves cap; examines hydraulic press; trapped in press.
1:30 am – 3:30 am or 4:00 am	Escapes losing thumb in process. Fire started as a result of lamp being crushed by press. Falls to ground, faints and is unconscious for a "very long time." Regains consciousness near Eyford train station, and makes a tourniquet with his handkerchief and a twig.
4:00 am -6:15 am	Finds way to Eyford train station; takes train to Reading; and then another train to Paddington Station.
6:50 am	At Paddington Station, Hatherley is approached by a guard, and taken to Watson's surgery.
6:50 am – 8:00 am	Watson dresses Hatherley's wound and listens to his story; cap reappears; and Hatherley feels great! – "Capital!"
8:00 am – 8:20 am	Watson and Hatherley take a cab to Baker Street.
8:20 am	Hatherley recounts events to Sherlock Holmes; has breakfast of fresh rashers and eggs.
9:00 am	Sherlock Holmes and Watson take Hatherley to Scotland Yard.
10:00 am – 1:00 pm	Sherlock Holmes, Watson, Inspector Bradstreet, Plain Clothes Policeman, and Hatherley take trains to Eyford. On train to Eyford, Inspector Bradstreet uses compass to draw a ten mile radius on the map of Eyford area.

They Went That a Way!!! Or, What's Burning Over Yonder?

What is more than interesting is before arriving at Eyford, four men look at a map to discern where the house is located and each gives a different direction:

Victor Hatherley – East
Plain Clothes Policeman – West
Dr. Watson – North
Sherlock Holmes – Center

1:00 pm   The four men arrive in Eyford. House in the distance is burning and smoke is rising.

"As we rolled into Eyford Station we saw a gigantic column of smoke which

streamed up from behind a small clump of trees in the neighbourhood and

hung like an immense ostrich feather over the landscape."

The House must be made of super fire resistant materials since it was burning longer than 12 hours and is still visible despite firemen on the scene and three fire engines.

Victor Hatherley's Traits – Talk About Being Fit!

The man is unbelievable to endure such a journey both back and forth, have a severed thumb, and still remain conscious during the harrowing escapades. Let's examine the traits that he exhibits in this story.

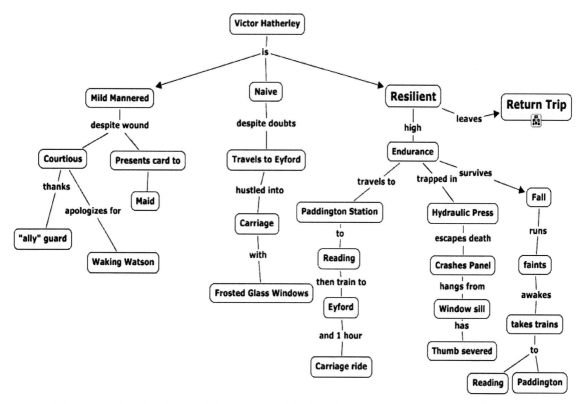

Victor Hatherley is a mild mannered individual. Despite his wound and severed thumb he thanks the guard, and then upon arriving at Dr. Watson's residence he presents his card to the maid and apologizes to Dr. Watson for waking him. He is somewhat naïve to have left for Eyford without knowing the full details and circumstances of the journey. His suspicions must have been aroused when he was put into a carriage with frosted windows. However, what must be said is that he is a highly resilient man. A review of the timeline of his ordeal and the story map attests to his durability and strength of mind. After all, how much blood can one lose and still recover, take a train to London and then return again to Eyford?

RETURN TRIP

Sherlock Holme, Dr. Watson,
Plain Clothes Policeman, Victor Hatherley

leave for

Return Trip

carriage to

Paddington Station

train back to

Reading

change train to

Eyford

This story is not without questions that prompt discussion. Some questions to be considered are:

1. Why is the hydraulic press built on the second floor?

   - How was it built without the neighbors noticing?

2. Notice the illustration. Is it possible for a thumb to be severed from the other digits' given the location of the hand?

3. How is it that there is a sliding panel leading to a passage-way from within the press?

4. How does Hatherley's cap reappear on Watson's books when his wound is being dressed?

5. In what other story does Sherlock Holmes match the correct metals (copper and zinc) with the coiners?

6. Why didn't Hatherley go to the police station three miles from Eyford?

7. Why doesn't the guard at Paddington Station take Hatherley to nearby St. Mary's Hospital?

8. How is it that the Thumb is found on the window-sill hours after the house is still burning?

9. Is this the most fire resistant house in memory?

10. Why doesn't Holmes pursue Colonel Lysander Stark, Mr. Ferguson, and Elise?

11. What is the meaning of Holmes' advice to Hatherley in the following dialogue?

Hatherley: "I have lost my thumb and I have lost fifty-guinea fee, and what have I gained?"

Holmes: "Experience"

Discussion

As can be deduced, in addition to the many questions that arise, there are also several theories that can be proposed regarding the events of the story. Professor Jay Finley Christ offers his theory as to the circumstances that involve Victor Hatherley and his fate.[111] He mentions a conversation with a correspondent who believes the person in the story was Mr. Jeremiah Hayling, an engineer, who had disappeared a year earlier and was summoned to Eyford. He caught his hand in the hydraulic press, and was able to escape after a fire started. It is surmised that Hayling invented the story of where he had been for a year in an effort to conceal his whereabouts.

Mr. Bliss Austin writes a very fine essay concerning the exploits of Victor Hatherley and the circumstances of the story itself.[112] His comments regarding the counterfeiting materials are enlightening. He notes that the firemen do not find a supply of mercury which is a necessary ingredient in the amalgamation of coins. Although both nickel and tin is mentioned in the story, Austin states that coins could not have been "an amalgam of nickel or tin, because the former does not amalgamate with mercury at all, and the latter does so to such a limited extent that it would be of little use for this purpose."

I contend that Colonel Lysander Stark had no intention to have Victor Hatherley return to London. He chose Hatherley carefully based on his lack of notoriety, an orphan and a bachelor. While he was busy preparing the wagon, Elise and Dr. Becher carried Hatherley nearer to Eyford train station. Why his wound was not addressed, given the loss of blood, is uncertain. Sherlock Holmes did not pursue the three because he knew that the coins could not be circulated given the metallurgical components. It would have been relatively easy for Sherlock Holmes to find three people, a beautiful woman Elise, Dr. Becher aka Mr. Ferguson an Englishman, and the villain Colonel Lysander Stark aka Fritz given their appearance, ethnic and gender makeup, and a heavy cart laden with large boxes traveling across a sparsely populated area. In fact, it is more likely that a wheel or an axle from the cart may have broken from the weight.

---

[111] Jay Finley Christ, "Thumbs Up, Thumbs Down," *Sherlock Holmes Journal*, vol. 2, no. 1 (July, 1954): 41-42.

[112] Bliss Austin, "Thumbing His Way to Fame," *Baker Street Journal*. vol. 1. no. 4. (October, 1946): 424-432.

Sherlock Holmes Revealed in Art

"Art in the blood is liable to take the strangest forms."

(The Greek Interpreter)

Eric Conklin, a trompe l' oeil artist, has created several paintings with hidden meanings associated with the Sherlock Holmes stories. Trompe l'oeil is the art of deception and is a form that displays realistic persons, places and objects with the intent of masking underlying meanings. The objects should be of actual or near actual size of the original item. The painting below was purchased by the Sherlock Holmes Museum in London and has also appeared on the cover of Umberto Echo's book, *The Name of the Rose*, the European edition distributed in Austria, Germany and Switzerland.[113]

SOURCE: Reprinted by permission of the artist, Eric Conklin, USA,
(www.ericconklin.com)

---

[113] This original painting is realistic and in color. This link shows the painting in color www.ericconklin.com/sherlockholmes1.html

Visual Thinking

Within the painting are clues that need to be unraveled in order to identify a famous saying that occurs in one of the stories. You may find it interesting to take a few minutes to examine the painting carefully. Make a list of the contents. Do these items reveal any clues? Can you make sense of them? Does a particular story come to mind? If you can solve the name of the story, you will be able to find the saying that is the name of the painting.

By answering these questions you are engaging in the process of visual thinking.[114] Visual thinking demands:

> "...the ability to find meaning in imagery. It involves a set of skills ranging
> from simple identification (naming what one sees) to complex interpretation
> on contextual, metaphoric and philosophical levels. Many aspects of cognition
> are called upon, such as personal association, questioning, speculating, analyzing,
> fact-finding, and categorizing. Objective understanding is the premise of much of
> this literacy, but subjective and affective aspects of knowing are equally important."

Rudolf Arnheim wrote a seminal book, *Visual Thinking*, which requires us to go beyond passive reasoning to an active process of using imagery to process the conceptual properties of an art form. Arnheim argued, "the remarkable mechanisms by which the senses understand the environment are all but identical with the operations described by the psychology of thinking."[115]

---

[114] Philip Yenawine, "Thoughts on Visual Literacy." In James Flood, Shirley Brice Heath, and Diane Lapp, *Handbook of Research on Teaching Literacy through the Communicative and Visual Arts* (Macmillan Library Reference, 1997).
[115] Rudolf Arnheim, *Visual Thinking* (London: Faber and Faber, 1969), Preface v.

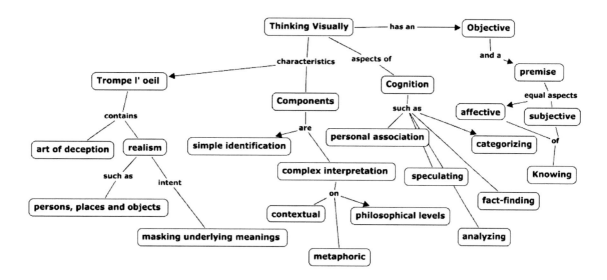

The concept map above shows the various aspects that encompass thinking visually when analyzing an art form. Trompe l' oeil artists encompass these characteristics in their paintings and include the art of deception and realism such as persons, places, and objects with the intent of masking underlying meanings. Also similar components include simple identification and complex interpretation on contextual, metaphoric, and philosophical levels. Cognitive reasoning processes such as personal association, speculating, analyzing, fact-finding, and categorizing are significant aspects of the thinking visually process. The objective of thinking visually has as its premise equal affective and subjective aspects of knowing.

When creating a work of art, such the painting by Eric Conklin that is being examined, it is incumbent on us to use our intellectual cognition in order to abstract the deeper meaning that the artist intended. The process of intellectual cognition described by Rudolph Arnheim is shown below:

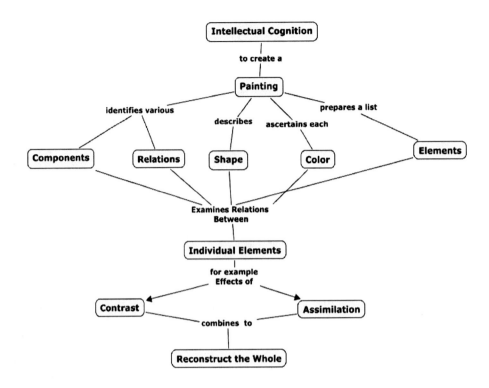

This process is used by a viewer/reader of the painting when abstracting the artist's rendition and deciphering the images and symbols that go beyond their literal meaning. The artist constructs the painting; the viewer/reader of the painting deconstructs and forms a meaningful interpretation. This requires taking the parts that are represented and deconstructing them to achieve an overall schematic of understanding that goes beyond simple identification. As Rudolph Arnheim states, "The work of art is an interplay of vision and thought."[116]

Just as readers rely on their prior knowledge and world experience when trying to comprehend a text, the same processes are used when viewing a painting. It is this organized knowledge that is accessed during reading or viewing that is referred to as schema (plural schemata). Readers and viewers make use of their schema when they can relate what they already know about a topic to the facts and ideas appearing in a text or a visual representation. The richer the schema is for a given topic the better a reader/viewer will understand the topic. The more one knows about Sherlock Holmes the better the person is able to relate this knowledge and give meaning to the images of the painting. During this process visual thinking combines with intellectual knowledge to bridge complex percepts by simplifying them; thereby, creating a fuller understanding

---

[116] Arnheim, 273.

of the artist's intention. In this painting, the artist has created the work using images and symbols as clues to evoke the viewer/reader's interest and intellect to decipher its meaning.

Reading a Painting

Images shown in the painting serve as symbols that depict meaning. The complexity given to them by the artist overlaps the reality of the symbol and its meaning within a context that encompasses the world of Sherlock Holmes. An image is a sign that shows regularity in events and objects. The images are both literal and interpretive and combine to provide the necessary application to decipher its meaning. They serve as clues to guide us in the quest for a resolution. As in the modes of reading comprehension, these processes need to be considered when reading a painting:

1. What does the artist say through this work?
2. What does the artist mean by the images, signs and symbols as clues?
3. How can I apply and reconstruct these meanings to form an understanding?

Eric Conklin uses these images, signs, and symbols, at different levels of abstraction. The literal which is a lower level; the interpretive, which transforms into a high order of comprehension by deciphering; and, the applied level of abstraction that takes the implied meaning to a higher level of abstraction by applying it to the story and its message. The successful viewer/reader has now unmasked and revealed the hidden meaning of the painting.

In an effort to simplify complexity we must first decipher the images that contain the primary clues. These images include the candle, book, and magnifying glass and where it is focused. We also need to consider the context in which this painting is to be viewed. It is a Sherlock Holmes story that evokes our prior knowledge about what we already know about Sherlock Holmes' characteristics, disguises, physical features, wearing apparel, and the setting of the historical period. The images of the painting – the pipe, the magnifying glass, the candle, and the note serve as stimuli to activate our prior knowledge that enables the reasoning processes to begin.

We invoke the processes of thinking visually by revealing the uncertainty; making the complex simple. We do this by interpreting and unmasking the images, first identifying those images that we recognize and then grounding the factors that are portrayed by bridging the gap of what we already know to what needs to be understood. This process involves analyzing, sorting, discarding, and threading relevant clues that lead to a meaningful resolution.

Backward Mapping

Sherlock Holmes uses the process of backward mapping when solving his cases. He analyzes the facts that have occurred and traces and sorts through them toward a resolution. Taking this stance, let's use this method to decipher the painting's clues leading to its meaning. Did your list have these: the opened page of the book; the magnifying glass; the candle; the crossword puzzle; the hourglass and timepiece; and, the pipe?

The Book

A careful review of the opened page of the book indicates that the story is from *The Return of Sherlock Holmes*. A question arises, "Which one?" We now need to find which clues appear in a story appearing in *The Return*.

The Magnifying Glass

Focuses on the book's title.

The Candle

The candle is a significant clue to the story and the naming of the painting. The candle signifies not only the revelation of light in the darkness, but also the need for urgency. Sidney Paget's drawing in this painting portrays Holmes holding a candle and dramatically arousing Watson to accompany him on a case of interest.[117] The shaking of Watson is another indicator of the need to leave the premises in haste. The candle signifies the early morning time in which this event takes place and the exigency of the matter since Watson is surprised with this unusual arousal. And, of course, it occurred "on a bitterly cold and frosty morning, towards the end of winter of '97."

---

[117] Walter Klinefelter, *Sherlock Holmes in Portrait and Profile.* (New York: Schocken Books, 1975), 58. He states that two drawings from *The Return of Sherlock Holmes* "are among the finest that Paget made of Sherlock Holmes." One portrays Holmes in fisticuffs, in *The Solitary Cyclist*; the other this one in *The Adventure of the Abbey Grange*.

"The candle in his hand shone upon his eager, stooping face, and told me at a glance that something was amiss."

Scott Bond's drawing depicts a similar scene whereby it is Watson who awakens Holmes on a matter of modern day importance. Again the candle signifies the early time of morning and the seriousness of the awakening.[118] So too, is the similar tugging of Holmes' and the use of the exclamation point.

"Get up and on the case Holmes, or you'll be replaced by an Internet consulting firm!"

---

[118] Scott Bond, "Art in the Blood," Baker Street Journal, vol. 51, no. 2 (Summer, 2001): 47. Reprinted with permission of the artist.

Crossword Puzzle

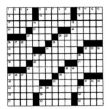

The crossword puzzle shown in the painting implies an image of mystery. It suggests that in order to solve the hidden meaning of the painting, it will be necessary to crack the code. It signals a problem or question that needs attention in order to understand the painting's hidden meaning. It brings to mind words and their meaning. The arrangement of the letters to form words and meaningful completions are of paramount importance. This notion bridges to words on a page such as a note. It is this clue that needs to be considered when simplifying the complexity of the painting.

A Note or Two: Holmes drew a note from his pocket, and read aloud?

> 'Abbey Grange, Marsham, Kent,
>
> '3:30 A.M.

'MY DEAR MR. HOLMES:

I should be very glad of your immediate assistance in what promises to be a most remarkable case. It is something quite in your line. Except for releasing the lady I will see that everything is kept exactly as I have found it, but I beg you not to lose an instant, as it is difficult to leave Sir Eustace there.

> 'Yours faithfully,
> 'STANLEY HOPKINS.

Second Note:

There was a pond in the park, and to this my friend led the way. It was frozen over, but a single hole was left for the convenience of a solitary swan. Holmes gazed at it, and then passed on to the lodge gate. There he scribbled a short note for Stanley Hopkins, and left it with the lodge-keeper.

The hour glass, timepiece and pipe

> He had lit his pipe and held his slippered feet to the cheerful blaze of the fire.
> Suddenly he looked at his watch.
> "I expect developments, Watson."
> "When?"
> "Now–within a few minutes. I dare say you thought I acted rather badly to
> Stanley Hopkins just now?"

Taken together, some clues are more important than others. In this case, they lead to identifying the Sherlock Holmes story, "The Adventure of the Abbey Grange," with the added illustration and accompanying remark that names the painting: "The Games Afoot." Uttering the words that have been often repeated in writings and screenplays, "Come, Watson, come! The game is afoot." The urgency of the statement is emphasized by an exclamation point. In an earlier essay, "Simplifying Complexity in Sherlock Holmes Stories," I stated that complexity this side of simple is complex. However, simplicity the other side of complexity is "simple." Simple because what may have been once complex is now meaningful and understood.

An Interview with the Artist

I asked Eric Conklin to answer a few questions about this painting. The responses are as follows:

Q.   What prompted the idea to paint Sherlock Holmes?

A.   As a Trompe l'Oeil artist it is engrained in us to give more to a painting than just a pretty picture. In most cases I strive to give a satirical underlining meaning to the painting for the viewers enjoyment. As a fan of Sherlock Holmes mysteries, the idea was fresh to apply the meaning of the mystery to a painting that gave the viewer a little more to do than just view the painting; it made a foundation for the viewer to explore the painting beyond the image alone. Seventeen century Dutch artists did something very similar; they painted images of the 'five senses' that gave the viewer the opportunity to recognize what they were. My very first interactive painting was imagery that depicted 'six senses'. At the same time the movie (starring Bruce Willis) the "Six Sense" came out, my painting of the six senses had nothing to do with the movie but people made a connection and it became one of the favorites in the exhibit. I then thought that maybe viewers were looking for something more than just a painting that would satisfy only their visual needs, maybe they needed something to stir their analytical needs as well. So, the first 'mystery painting' was born.

Q.   What was the source of the background information that you accessed?

A.   I have a book titled; The Original Illustrated Sherlock Holmes by Authur Conan Doyle, Castle Books, Edison, New Jersey. While reading the Adventure of the Abbey Grange, I thought that it would make a good introduction to the first series of the Sherlock Holmes Mystery paintings. I also use my computer for research and development, Google is a great source.

Q.   How did you decide on the images for the paintings?

A.   In my research for all paintings, I purchase props to exacting standards. As a collector of art, I've found that I could purchase (when possible) period pieces that not only add to my collection but will appreciate in value as I hold on to them. With Sherlock Holmes there are certain items that are associated with him and that are depicted in Doyle's stories and Sidney Paget's illustrations. These are all 19th century pieces;

Deerstalker cap – from Piccadilly Street London
Meerschaum pipe with case
Gold Watch
Measuring tape
Bobbie's whistle
Several magnifying classes
French National Order of the Legion of Honours, medal
Oil handheld lamp
16th – 19th century leather bound books
Brass candle sticks of various styles
Brass compass
And of course the iconic Stradivarius violin

I keep these items in one place and arrange the items as they appear in the story. If there is something that is iconic to the story and I don't have it…I'll get it.

Q.   Colors?

A.   My art training was in the traditional style of the Old Dutch Masters, mostly Rembrandt's era. You'll find that their use of chiaroscuro was prominent in most of their paintings and the 'dark to light' gave a very dramatic feel or mood to their paintings. As mysteries tend to be dramatic it seemed appropriate to use the dark colors of the Old Masters to set the mood of the Sherlock Holmes Mystery paintings.

Q.   How were the images of the painting arranged conceptually to reveal a hidden message?

A.   The props in the painting were arranged using a process known as the Golden Mean. It is a mathematical calculation that arranges items to be more aesthetic to the eye. Originally used by the Greeks in architecture and modeling of the figures for their Pagan gods. In my paintings I make small adjustments to the items to make finding the clues easier, but always keeping the mathematical arrangement the same. Each item in the painting either has a meaning or supports an object of meaning. Additional items are left out to not confuse the viewer.

Q.   How did you know when to reach closure?

A.   This is the best question and one that is asked of artists with many answers. To me the painting is finished when it feels complete. I hang the painting in my studio in such a way that it is the first thing that I see in the morning. In doing this I see it with fresh eyes every time. As I approach the work it will feel complete or not. If it's complete, I won't go any further. If it feels incomplete I'll wait a few days to see if something develops that will enhance the painting. I have currently a set-up for a new Sherlock Holmes Mystery painting; it's been set up for a year and a half and I now think it's ready to be painted.

Paintings and drawings add to the story by providing a context for the reader to stir the imagination. The clothes, the steam engine, the compartment car, the hansom cab, the streets, the moor, the hound, and so forth engage us with the events described and the surrounding social, political, and cultural conditions that prevailed during the period. This painting that has been analyzed is at a higher level of abstraction than its visual appearance. In this painting, Eric Conklin has intentionally drawn images to promote a higher level of mental processing requiring interpretation and application.

Knowing the characteristics of a trompe l' oeil artist prepares us to sort through the images to reveal the hidden intentions so that a deeper meaning can be achieved. The notion is to reach congruence with the artist's message and intent by viewing the colors, shapes, place, and position in a painting. When we grasp a meaning not our own or when we are able to make sense of the artist's message we achieve felt significance. This is a powerful moment in educating when a grasped meaning and feeling the sensation simultaneously come together. In this instance, we exclaim, "I get it!" "I understand!" We have unraveled the hidden message, pieced together the clues, and made our way toward resolving the uncertainty. Taking a painting and letting it lie in its fallow state is an injustice to the artist and to us. Once its meaning is grasped, not only is our mental model enriched, but a level of appreciation with the work is attained that provides us with a sense of educational worth.

Appendix

Visual Literacy Guide

A visual literacy guide is an adjunct aid used to focus learners with a visual portrayal such as a painting, illustration, photograph, figure, table, graph and so forth. In this instance, the guide relates to Eric Conklin's painting in this essay. Two levels of comprehension are used: literal and interpretive.

Directions: Place a check mark before the words you see in the painting. Add one of your own.

_____ magnifying glass   _____ cap

_____ books   _____ candle

_____ note   Add One _____

Directions: Place a check mark before the words that you believe tell about the painting. Add one of your own words. Be able to explain your selections.

_____ mystery   _____ tranquil   _____ realistic

_____ imaginative   _____ abstractness   _____ deceptive

_____ action   Add One _____

Directions: Read each statement below. If you agree with the statement place a check mark before it. If you disagree, do not check it. Be able to give reasons for your selections. Write a statement of your own.

_____ 1. The painting represents, "art for art's sake"

_____ 2. Interpreting the images and symbols within the context of what you know about Sherlock Holmes is important.

_____ 3. No matter how hard you try, it is not possible to reveal the hidden message of this painting.

_____ 4. Relating what you already know about Sherlock Holmes' characteristics to this painting, will lead to a resolution of the story's meaning.

_____ 5. Your turn to write a statement _____

Sherlock Holmes, American Football, and Schenectady

Source: Photograph of the Union College football team in an 1887
Scrapbook courtesy of Special Collections in Schaffer Library at
Union College, Schenectady, New York.

I

"Lovely scenery along this Hudson Valley landscape Holmes, with the autumn leaves showing their brilliant shades of color." "Yes, Watson, it brings back memories." "Memories, Homes!" "Ah, Watson I believe I told you about the lecture tour organized by Major Pond that took me to thirty towns and cities. At that time we traveled by rail through this same beautiful countryside. It was on that occasion that we stopped in Schenectady to deliver an address." "Sch...ah...what?" "Schenectady, Watson. The Electric City. The city where the great American inventor Thomas Edison founded the General Electric Company, and where the steam engine built by the American Locomotive Works makes our travel most pleasurable. The city that first introduced me to American football where the ball is kicked and thrown." "Don't you mean Rugby?" "Football, Watson." "A game where players from each team gather along a scrimmage line to do battle." "Do they use weapons?" "Never mind Old Fellow." "Let's take in the view of the rolling hills.

II

Although I had several questions, I could tell by the look in my companion's face that he was far-away, absorbed in times gone past. Of course, it never bothered him when intruding on my thoughts. On our way along the Erie Canal the train pulled into the next station. The conductor called, "Schenectady." "All out for Schenectady." "Quick Watson, let's get off." It was a bit impulsive, but we gathered our belongings and disembarked onto the platform. It was a sunny, but crisp autumn day. Not a cloud in the sky. Holmes quickly began walking toward the street.

"Where are we going Holmes?" Holmes was silent for a moment. He looked from left to right and then said, "We are going the few blocks to visit Union College founded in 1795." I was unacquainted with the college, but thought there must be something brewing if it had captured Holmes' interest. It was a lovely setting for a college: small, but picturesque. As we walked the grounds we saw the statute of Chester A. Arthur, an American president who had graduated from this college, class of 1848. We saw the ivy covered buildings, and then we came upon a large athletic field crowded with people. Something was about to begin. People were filling the stands looking for seats with a good view. Suddenly, Holmes paused and became pensive. A few moments passed and he spoke more to himself than to me, "A Union College football player died in a game against New York University." He turned to me and said, "I remember that the circumstances sparked a wave of sentiment among some college presidents with a call to abandon the game entirely. As I recall, President Roosevelt intervened resulting in regulations concerning the use of headgear and other safety features that were introduced to make the game less brutal as well as making changes in the rules of the game itself. What say you Watson! Shall we take in the game?" I must say that my curiosity was aroused.

As we came closer, I noticed that the players on the field wore heavy padding under their shirts. Their trousers were also bulging and they wore shoes with spikes protruding from the soles. Most unusual was the headgear they wore. Astonishingly there were two poles with a bar across forming the letter "H" standing upright from the ground at either end of the field. I paused... thought for a minute...then another... and finally reconciled that this "H" was not intended as a greeting for my friend. After all, we ourselves did not know we were coming to Sch... Sch.... to this place. I could tell that Holmes was interested and keenly observed the warm-up by the players. Nothing escaped his senses. I followed his gaze at the players observing his every glance. First he looked at the knees of their trousers. Immediately I thought of Spaulding, but I would not be swayed from my focus.[119] He too, observed their padded shirts, spiked shoes, and heavy hats. The dry field made the surface the consistency of hard packed clay.

---

[119] A reference to Vincent Spaulding aka John Clay in Arthur Conan Doyle's, *The Red-Headed League*.

III

Several players met at the middle of the field with a man smartly dressed wearing a striped shirt, white trousers, stockings, and a white cap. I asked, "What are they doing?" Holmes replied that the referee was meeting with the captains of each team and they would engage in a coin toss to determine who would receive the ball first. It was a preliminary ritual that occurred now, as it did then, when the first football game was played on this field in 1886. As the game progressed, I refrained from asking questions, since it was evident that Holmes was immersed in the play of the combatants. As I watched, I thought about my friend's methods. In my mind I heard his words, "Always look at the hands first, Watson. Then cuffs, trouser-knees, and boots."[120] It was then that I was determined to show him that with observation and deduction one could easily explain the happening on the field of play.

IV

I watched for fifteen minutes until an official blew a whistle. Again, I carefully honed in on the players hands, then their cuffs, noticing their trouser-knees, and finally their boots. After another fifteen minute period the official again blew his whistle stopping play; whereby, the players ran off the field into a shed at the end of the north side. "Well, Watson what do you think of American football?" It was my turn to show what I could do. "Holmes, I have been watching closely the players on the field and am somewhat confident in my interpretation of what has happened to this juncture."

"Pray tell, Watson!" "What enlightenment can you shed so far?" I was used to Holmes' smugness. His superior, know-it-all attitude. A tone in his voice that was more condescending than accepting. A facial expression that reflected a stone-carving of the wind sculpture before blowing on the unsuspecting man in the Aesop fable. I demurred until the beginning of the second half so as to better illustrate my methods of observation. Meanwhile, we both watched and listened to the band as it played contemporary and classical medleys to which he hummed along and was quick to name each piece along with the composer. Thankfully halftime finally came to a close.

V

The second half began, and it was my turn to show Holmes that this American game of football could easily be mastered in one sitting. As the third quarter progressed,

---

[120] *The Adventure of the Creeping Man.*

108

the team which I had been observing lined up. However, the opposing home team called a time out and both teams ran to the sideline to converse with their respective coaches. Seizing this lull in the action, I nonchalantly said in a matter-of-fact tone, "Interesting formation don't you think?" At first, Holmes looked to his right and then turned around to see where the voice had originated. Then, he looked at me and said, "Oh, Watson so it is you!" "Yes, indeed it is a formidable formation." Not deterred, I continued. "Let me make a few observations." "First, did you notice the hands of the man in backfield? They are taped. You will notice that the team with the ball has soiled uniforms particularly at the knees, chest, and back of their shirts. Finally, look carefully at the extra-long spikes the players are wearing." "Excellent Watson." "There is no doubt you have noted the finer points of this particular offensive team. What, then, do you deduce from your findings?"

It was now that I would impress Holmes with how rudimentary knowledge can be expanded into funded knowledge once my deductive methods were revealed. His smugness would turn to surprise, his voice would spontaneously utter shrieks of amazement, and his stone-like facial expression of Aesop's wind sculpture would turn into one of pensive wonder.

"Well, Holmes, I examined the formation composed of the players and thought they are planning to run the ball. This was further confirmed by the seven men on the line, two of which were spread out on either side of the formation seven yards each. As I stated, the player in the backfield has his hands taped. This can only mean better protection when getting and running with the ball. The soiled trouser-knees and the front and back shirts indicate that these linemen are exerting their strength upon their opponents attempting to drive them off the ball in order to make it easier for the player with the ball to gain territory. The fact that the players' boots have extra long cleats provide the obvious clue that in order to get better traction, these cleats have an advantage over their opponents who have smaller, less protruding ones."

"You astound me, Watson." Once again you prove my axiom that, "There is nothing more deceptive than an obvious fact."[121] Or that, "Intense mental concentration has a curious way of blotting out what has passed."[122] How about, ... "Please Holmes. Enough of the story quotes." "Permit me one more, "You mean well, Watson. Shall I demonstrate your own ignorance?"[123]

---

[121] *The Boscombe Valley Mystery.*
[122] *The Hound of the Baskervilles.*
[123] *The Adventure of the Dying Detective.*

VI

Now was the time that I dreaded the most. A time when smugness turned to annoyance; when tone of voice and demeanor evoked instances of previously encountered circumstances; and, when facial expressions influenced body movements like a professor addressing an impoverished student.[124] Under the gaze of surrounding patrons, he began. "First, Watson, let's examine this formation with two wide receivers. It is unlikely that a running play will occur given the lack of men available to block for the halfback and also the fact that the down and distance is such that one would have to run eighteen yards in order to reach the yardage for a new set of downs or, as you might say, opportunities. Second, the player with the taped hands is unlikely to run with the ball even if he intended to do so. The thickness of the tape wrapping would make it extremely difficult for the player to hold onto the ball once he was tackled. You were astute to notice the soiled trouser-knees and the shirts both front and back. The soiled knees are from their being beaten down by the opposing linemen. However, you neglect to account for the shape of the soiled areas. A more attentive view shows that these players have footprints outlined on the front of their shirts. Take this fact and associate it with the soiled back of their shirts, and it can be deduced that the combatants from the other side are not only knocking them down, but more snappishly are running over them while they are on their backs – thus the footprints. Lastly, the use of extra long cleats. They are not, as you said with some certainty, for gaining more traction. In fact, you may have noticed these players slipping when they run due to the dryness of the field. Players wear extra long cleats when the weather is inclement and the ground muddy. As I have stated, the sky is clear and devoid of rain clouds." "So, Watson," "If we combine these clues, the tape on the hands, the soiled knees and shirts, and the linemen wearing inappropriate long cleats, together with the score 52-0 in favor of their opponent, a reasonable assumption can be made that this team is not prepared and that the game's outcome is foreseeable."

VII

When the applause dwindled and Holmes had acknowledged these admirers with a casual nodding of his head and a flick of the hand, the rest of the game proceeded without any conversation between us. As the gun sounded ending the game I took solace, with some regret, that it was not pointed at me. Introspectively, I knew that this American football experience was another in a long line of embarrassing moments spent with Holmes.

---

[124] *The Adventure of the Dancing Men*; also, *The Yellow Face.*

VIII

After the game, we resumed our tour of the campus and later made our way to a cabstand. "Watson, will you hail a cab to a hotel?" "Certainly." As the cab pulled alongside I asked Holmes, "What is the name of the hotel?" "Hotel Schenectady," he replied. Startled, I said out loud, "Hotel Sch...ah...what?" The cab driver shook his head and looked away.

I muttered to myself, "It never ends."

(But then again, do we want it to?)

PART 2

IN THE FOOTSTEPS

This past summer in July and August of 2011 my wife, Vicki, and I followed the footprints left by some of the incidents portrayed in the Sherlock Holmes stories. We were scheduled for a conference in Belgium and I had received approval by Clare Hopkins, archivist at Trinity College, Oxford, to view Monsignor Ronald Knox's papers. These original manuscripts and the *Gryphon Book of Minutes* were made available by Sharon Cure, the librarian. A few minutes' walk to Merton College from our hotel and a meeting with Julian Reid, archivist, provided more information. A series of planned events prior to our Oxford stay enabled us to imprint our own footprints along the paths of Sherlock Holmes. We followed them at Reichenbach Falls, visited the Sherlock Holmes Museum in Meiringen Switzerland, and traveled to Trummelbach Falls, prior to journeying to Oxford.

In this section, two essays of a travelogue nature are presented. One essay compares Reichenbach Falls and Trummelbach Falls. Second, is our visit to Trinity College at Oxford to view the Monsignor Ronald A. Knox papers and the *Gryphon Club Book of Minutes*.

Footprints Along the Paths:

Reichenbach Falls and Trummelbach Falls

> "There is no branch of detective science which is so important and so much neglected as the art of tracing footsteps."
>
> (A Study in Scarlet)

In this essay background is given for Conan Doyle's selection of Reichenbach Falls for Sherlock Holmes and Professor Moriarty's demise, and a comparison is made between the physical characteristics of Reichenbach Falls and Trummelbach Falls. Reichenbach Falls as the setting for "The Final Problem" is certainly dramatic. But, Trummelbach Falls may have provided an even more spectacular venue given the force of the water, the internal caverns, and the atmosphere surrounding the setting for the end!

Reichenbach Falls

Background

The Reichenbach Falls setting was no accident. Conan Doyle had visited the falls with his ailing wife Louise. The purpose of the journey was to provide an environment that would enable her to cure her illness. Instead, her disease worsened. Returning to London, Doyle consulted a lung specialist and Louise was diagnosed as having consumption a debilitating and fatal disease. Doyle blamed himself for not taking more time to care for his wife. He pointed to the time he devoted to writing the Sherlock Holmes stories that interfered with him being with Louise. This became a major impact on his decision to terminate Sherlock Holmes.

As a young adolescent, Conan Doyle was encouraged by his mother to read many books. One that was particularly influential was Mayne Reid's, *The Scalp Hunters* (1851). Reid, a fur trapper and trader in America, was once a tutor. This book, written in the first person, inspired Doyle to later write using first person as a storytelling technique, and served as an impetus to learn botany. Charles Higham writes that the passage, reprinted below, evoked memories when Conan Doyle was writing, "The Final Problem" of the scene depicted at Reichenbach Falls.[125]

> I stand upon beetling cliffs and look into chasms that yawn beneath,
>
> Sleeping in the silence of desolation…. Dark precipices frown me
>
> into fear, and my head reels with a dizzy faintness.

Writing about the incident at Reichenbach Falls, Charles Higham tells of the curious departure of Dr. Watson. He had been called to Davos to aid a lady who was hemorrhaging as a result of consumption. There was no lady and the intent of the message was to distract Watson and lead him away from the falls. Contrary to the popular notion that Conan Doyle tired of writing about Sherlock Holmes, Higham states that this incident is not without significance.[126]

> Quite subtly, Conan Doyle is giving us the important reason why
>
> Holmes had to be killed off: the consumptive Louise brought about
>
> the death of Holmes, simply because she required Conan Doyle's attention.
>
> By hitherto neglecting her for Holmes, he had, in the light of his own guilt
>
> feelings, helped to bring upon her a death sentence. The choice of the
>
> Reichenbach Falls as the setting for Holmes's "death" is, of course, quite
>
> deliberate, since the severe cold of the area above it had aggravated
>
> Louise's illness. Soon after, he took her to Davos, one more, in his life,
>
> reality fulfilled the presentiments of art.

It was when Conan Doyle decided to bring Sherlock Holmes back that I find interesting. When writing, "The Valley of Fear: Three Missing Words," I had included in the Notes section that Conan Doyle was friends with Samuel McClure, and provided stories to his magazine and contributed financially to keep the magazine in production.[127] Although Conan Doyle was offered a sum of a hundred pounds per

---

[125] Charles Higham, *The Adventures of Conan Doyle: The Life of the Creator of Sherlock Holmes.* (London: Hamish Hamilton, 1976). 28. Charles Higham has written biographies and is the son of Sir Charles Higham, M.P., who was a friend of Conan Doyle and a well-known publicist between the wars.

[126] Ibid.. 112-113.

[127] See Notes, "The Valley of Fear: Three Missing Words," in this volume.

thousand words by Greenhough Smith for the stories to appear in *The Strand*, it was Samuel S. McClure of *McClures Magazine* in New York, who gave him a check for five thousand dollars (the same amount loaned by Doyle some years earlier) for six stories. There was a condition, however, that Holmes had to have survived Reichenbach Falls.[128]

This backdrop, and the many events described at Reichenbach Falls, prompted a journey to Switzerland.

Meiringen and Reichenbach Falls

After taking a train from Brussels to Paris and then an airplane to Switzerland, we made Zurich our base. One of our train journeys took us to Meiringen and the Reichenbach Falls. We left Zurich by train to Luzern; changed trains on route to Meiringen and the Falls. As we pulled into the Meiringen train station, a sunny day turned somewhat grey with intermingled drizzle and hard rainfall – a foreshadowing of what was to come.

We left the train station, walked across the street, and took a bus a short distance to the bottom of the Reichenbach Falls. The bus driver knew exactly the stop we wanted. I didn't know then that the short dialogue in which we engaged would later provide a referent for both him and me. He dropped us off to begin our trek.

---

[128] Higham, 181.

We purchased our tickets at the booth at the base of the falls and boarded the funicular. Riding the railway car provided an extraordinary view of what was below and what was to come. As we approached and departed from our car the spray of the falls slightly dampened our clothes and careened against our faces. We were not deterred!

We looked down at the bottom of the falls and were taken in by the amount of water pouring down the side of the mountain. The water looked as if it filled a cavity, blue in color, and offered a glimpse into what could happen if one should plunge within its recesses.

Looking up the mountain at the falls we sensed that this was a place that was believable in the eyes of Conan Doyle for Sherlock Holmes to meet his end in "The Final Problem." The setting is spectacular and the sounds of the falls coupled with the changing winds and weather provide a backdrop for such an event to take place.

Walking the path upwards was a spiritual experience. As we climbed the path the waterfall became more intense and our footsteps became embedded in the soil as the climb became more challenging. The path was narrow and the rain kept us on guard. One could imagine the thoughts of both Holmes and Moriarty as each made his way along the cliffs for the anticipated combat. Vicki kept her spirits high and braved the elements. I was able to keep pace as we trudged up the path that presented us with glorious views of the falls and surrounding area. We were troopers.

At the departure point, we viewed photographs, one of which was the visit by the members of the Sherlock Holmes Society of London in 2005. We glanced across the way, up to the "star" marker that depicts where Holmes and Moriarty fought and were struck by its distance from the waterfalls.

Before boarding the funicular for our journey downward we took a last look at the valley below.

We began our trip downward along the steep embankment.

The fog and the rain provided a dismal, yet exciting backdrop to our memorable journey. When reaching the bottom of the funicular we departed and viewed the plaque of Sherlock Holmes.

Meiringen and the Sherlock Holmes Museum (Moriarty's presence felt).

The bus and familiar driver returned us to the town of Meiringen. I didn't know how much the bus driver would be appreciated when he had first taken us from the train station to the funicular and then back to the train station and the drop off point. Vicki and I made our way in the rain to the Sherlock Holmes Museum.

Upon arriving we were asked if we wanted to leave our coats or bags behind the counter. I reached for my backpack and was more than surprised that I was not carrying it. I knew that the camera with the chip of many photos was in the backpack along with a journal I had been keeping, and the return train tickets, so I was very concerned. I quickly walked back to the bus station across from the train station. I was not sure if I had left my bag on the funicular or on the bus. There were three buses parked at the station and I was able to inquire about the bus driver who drove us earlier and learned that he would be returning within twenty minutes.

As I waited I couldn't but wonder if there was some sort of misdeed that had occurred. I could not dismiss the thought that Professor Moriarty's spirit was lurking about to do mischievous deeds to unwary travelers. My missing packpack. A coincidence? His image was clear as I peered through the raindrops waiting for the bus to return.

I anxiously waited until the driver wheeled the bus into the station. Peering through the windshield wipers he saw me and gave the thumbs up. I knew then that my backpack was secure. He assured me that nothing was missing and that he knew I would be waiting for him. I thanked him profusely and returned to the Museum - looking over my shoulder as I walked.

The Museum contained many artifacts among which was a replica of Sherlock Holmes and Dr. Watson's room with items arranged meticulously so as to depict its furnishings. The plan of the room illustrates the painstaking efforts that were taken to create a room that corresponded with the descriptions given in the stories.

There were display cases in the museum containing uniforms and items from the era. Also photographs adorned the walls of the events depicted in the story. One interesting display was a certificate honoring Sherlock Holmes as a citizen of Meiringen.

Of course, a painting of the duel between Sherlock Holmes and Moriarty was on display.

As was a portrait of the literary agent: A. Conan Doyle.

Outside the museum the statue of Sherlock Holmes resides with a plaque that reads:

Homage To
Sherlock Holmes
Sculpture
John Doubleday 1988

The bronze statue portrays Sherlock Holmes in a pensive, yet energetic, mood ready to take on a case of interest. Or is he, like I was, pondering the misdeeds of the Professor?

Walking the streets of Meiringen one could imagine the hansom cabs that once traversed these avenues; now transitioned and replaced by the automobile. Some shops still retain the memories of times long ago; even hotels, such as the Das Hotel Sherlock Holmes, have references to Sherlock Holmes that lure today's travelers to their inns.

We returned to the train station for our return to Zurich. And so it was that a trip to Meiringen led to a spectacular view of the Falls, a wander through the town, a visit to the museum, and an encounter (perhaps imaginary) with the Professor.

Upon arriving at our hotel, I thought about the two persons on the funicular that told us about Trummelbach Falls. The gentleman was very enthusiastic about the caverns and the force of the waters. Given my almost misfortune of losing my backpack with essentials contained therein, I was somewhat skeptical of a subversive plot – perhaps planned by… an unkind professor. Despite some misgivings, we looked at the railway map and decided to leave the next day for Trummelbach Falls. We were enticed to visit this site since we were very impressed with the setting we had just experienced at the Reichenbach Falls.

Trummelbach Falls

Vicki and I left Zurich by train to Lauterbrunner via Berne and Interlaken. We then took a bus to Trummelbach Falls. The following photograph is a view from the bottom of the falls.

Upon arrival at this small village we entered the Trummelbach Falls cavern. There are ten caverns with rushing, swirling waters streaming down the winding caverns walls with sharp curvatures. The *Lonely Planet Guide* reports that inside the mountain up to 20,000L of water per second flows through potholes and ravines shaped by the swirling waters. We entered a tightly compacted elevator filled to capacity with other visitors and ascended within the walls to the sixth level of the cavern.

Departing and then walking upwards from within the cavern to the top of level ten offered many spectacular views of the different levels of the roaring waters crashing down within the winding crevices. This photograph of my wife, Vicki, and me give some indication of the hollows and crevices that serve as the backdrop for this spectacular falls

The falls have tremendous force and the sound of the waters flowing down emit a high pitch.

Each level provides dramatic views of the different aspects of the inner walls of the caverns. The force of the falls was heard and felt as we continued upward towards the top of the tenth level. One such opening, shown in the photograph below, shows the force of the water careening down within the cavern. The sound of the water and the view of the fast-paced waterfall is a sight to behold.

NOTE: This photograph was not converted from color and appears as it was
taken with a digital camera.

An example of the depths of the cavern and the visitors who make their way
along the tunnels is shown.

Multiple views of the different aspects of the flowing falls can be seen when traversing the levels of the falls.

After reaching the top level, we walked down all ten levels to the bottom of the falls. The rushing waters with their thunderous roar; swirling down the crevices and openings with the cavern was a sight to behold. Each level combined with sprays of water cast a hue of colors that painted the cavern walls.

The geological impression made by the rapidly flowing water provides an indelible mental image of the wonders of nature.

After our trek up and then down the mountain I was gratified that Vicki emerged unscathed.

Both the Reichenbach Falls and the Trummelbach Falls provide the visitor with different, and yet spectacular settings. Reichenbach Falls is an outside venture whereas Trummelbach Falls combines an inner with an outside venue.

A. Conan Doyle used the Reichenbach Falls as the backdrop to describe the harrowing cliffs with its narrow paths as the venue for "The Final Problem." Just as spectacular would have been the Trummelbach Falls as the setting for Holmes and Moriarty to meet and engage in their duel. I could imagine the wily professor's body careening down the twisting, swirling waters among the levels of the cavern, with the tremendous deafening force of the flowing waters moving him swiftly along its corridors.

The next day we packed our suitcases for London and another series of footprints to follow along the Sherlock Holmes Walk. We did indeed tread the streets of London and have photos to show our footprints. We viewed a trial at the Old Bailey, and were in the gallery for an emergency session of Parliament. Then we made our way to Trinity College at Oxford.[129]

_____

[129]Jim Hawkins posted our journey on the Nashville Scholars of the Three Pipe Problem website (http://www.nashvillescholars.net/) to Meiringen and the Reichenbach Falls, which generated some interest to those who read and viewed this event. Kay Blocker and Dean Richardson included it in the _Plugs and Dottles,_ Nashville Scholars of the Three-Pipe Problem, September 2011.

A Visit to Trinity College at Oxford and the Gryphon Book

       In July of 2000, my wife and I each presented a paper at St. Catherine's College in Oxford England.[130] We had visited Cambridge before coming to Oxford so we were very fortunate to have been in both university cities. My wife Vicki, a professor of language and literacy at Vanderbilt University, had made arrangements to meet with students from her university who were attending a semester of study at Homerton College at Cambridge. In previous years, I have visited the Toronto Public Library's Sherlock collection overseen by Peggy Perdue the librarian, and also the collection at the University of Minnesota. I met with Tim Johnson, Curator of Special Collections and Rare Books, and, through the kindness of Julie McKuras, was taken deep below into the stacks to wander through the rows of Sherlockian books, papers, and artifacts that are housed at this library. I must admit disappointment when told by Julie, that the *Beeton's Annual* that I was coveting was not a parting gift. Regardless, the chance to see these collections was very much appreciated as was the permission by Clare Hopkins, archivist, to view the Monsignor Ronald A. Knox papers and the *Gryphon Club Book* at Trinity College, Oxford.

---

[130] Marino C. Alvarez. "Explorers of the Universe: Electronic Literacy Environments," presented at the United Kingdom Reading Association, 36th Annual International Conference, St. Catherine's College ,Oxford, England, July 2000.

Visit to Trinity College Oxford

On August 16, 2011 my wife and I journeyed by an early train from London to Oxford. We had scheduled a one night's stay at the Old Bank Hotel and during these two days a visit to Trinity College. After checking into our hotel, we walked down Turl Street passing the Bodleian Library and the Bridge of Sighs onto Broad Street. Trinity College's main entrance is located on this main street among the cafes, shops, pubs, and Blackwell's Bookshop. Trinity College, founded in 1555, is situated in the center of Oxford, close to libraries, laboratories, lecture halls and all the city's amenities.

I had received prior approval by Clare Hopkins, archivist at Trinity College, Oxford, to view Monsignor Ronald Knox's papers. Upon our scheduled arrival we told the porter of the lodge and mentioned that we had made arrangements to meet Sharon Cure, the librarian. Within a few minutes Sharon met us and we were on our way to the library to view the Monsignor Knox collection. Since the academic year had not yet begun for the students, we had the library to ourselves.

The Library

Upon entering the library, I felt a sense of respect just as when I enter an antiquarian book store. Surrounded by these many works, I take time to reflect. For every book on an inch of a shelf are someone's thoughts and feelings within. They are revealed when the cover is opened and the ideas are read, understood, and their meaning imagined.

Washington Irving's "The Mutability of Literature," in *The Sketch Book*, depicts the trials of a book and its author and its influence over an indeterminate period. When describing old volumes spanning hundreds of years, on shelves of a library in a monastery he writes:

> How much, thought, has each of these volumes, now thrust aside with such
>
> indifference, cost some aching head! How many weary days! How many
>
> sleepless nights! How have their authors buried themselves in the solitude
>
> of cells and cloisters, shut themselves up from the face of man and the still
>
> more blessed face of nature, and devoted themselves to painful research
>
> and intense reflection! And all for what? To occupy an inch of dusty
>
> shelf --- to have the title of their works read now and then in a future age

by some drowsy churchman or casual straggler like myself, and in another

age to be lost, even to remembrance.[131]

And so it was that a straggler, though invited, but still a straggler was able to read a historical text of recorded minutes that occupied "an inch of dusty shelf" that few had read.

All was ready, the *Gryphon Club Book of Minutes* and the Reverend Ronald A. Knox's papers for examination.

Sharon Cure showed me the materials and I gingerly carried them to a corner desk for viewing. I first paged carefully through the papers, some of which were typewritten in large envelopes. Others were written in Latin in that the process was more of a perusal than a study. Although I found some of the papers in Latin typed neatly, my forte was not in deciphering their meaning. My main interest was reading the green book with gold lettering. When I opened the *Gryphon Club Book of Minutes*, I exerted an exegesis of concentration as they related to the presence of Father Knox. I had read the report of Nicholas Utechin who had visited the library and viewed this collection some months earlier.[132] His thorough analysis of the contents along with those

[131] Washington Irving, *The Sketch Book*. (New York: The New American Library of World Literature, Inc. 1961), 128-129.

[132]Nicholas Utechin, "From Piff-Pouff to Backnecke: Ronald Knox and 100 Years of 'Studies in the Literature of Sherlock Holmes,'" *The Baker Street Journal 2010 Christmas Annual*. Also, Nicholas

members present during Father Knox's reading of his paper are a must read. So, too is a book by Michael J. Crowe who provides insightful glimpses into Father Knox's writings.[133]

My intent is to write my experiences and impressions of this historical text, though not as complete and thorough as Nicholas Utechin's account. The first entry that drew my attention was the Rules of the Gryphon club.

Utechin, "The Case of the First Reading," *The Baker Street Journal*, vol. 61. no. 1 (Spring, 2011): 34-47.
[133] Michael J. Crowe, *Ronald Knox and Sherlock Holmes* (Indianapolis: Gasogene Books, 2011).

The Rules of the Gryphon Club

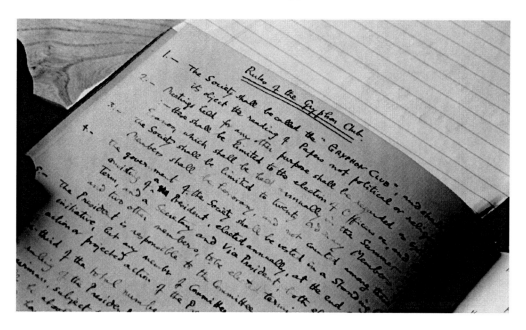

    The Rules of the Gryphon Club are recorded in the book. The double underlining indicates the degree of emphasis placed on these rules. The first rule states, "The society shall be called the "Gryphon Club", and shall have for its object the reading of Papers not political or religious." This rule established the tenor of what papers and books the club would not be discussing at their meetings. It seems clear that the intent of the meetings were to read, listen and discuss literary works that could be shared among its members. Further rules specified the purpose and function of the club, its officers and members.

    I focused my attention to the day that Father Knox read his paper in his room to a gathering of the members of the Gryphon Club and their visitors. The entry of the proceedings and the reading by Monsignor Knox of the paper, "Studies on Sherlock" was recorded as follows:

Father Knox's Reads "Studies on Sherlock Holmes"

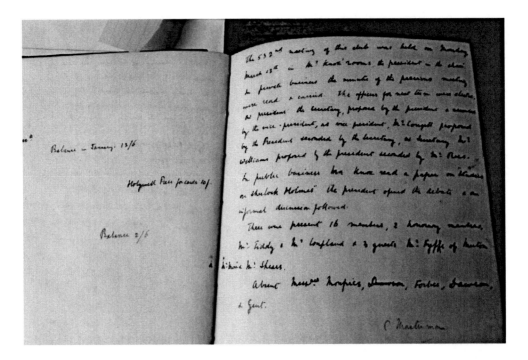

The 532nd meeting of the club was held on Monday March 13th in Mr. Knox' rooms, the president in the chair. In private business the minutes of the previous meeting were read & carried. The officers for next term were elected. As president the secretary, proposed by the president & seconded by the vice-president, as vice-president, Mr. Congill proposed by the president seconded by the secretary, as secretary Mr. Williams proposed by the president seconded by Mr. Rees. In public business Mr. Knox read a paper on "Studies on Sherlock Holmes" The president opened the debate & an informal discussion followed.

There were present 16 members, 2 honorary members, Mr. Tiddy & Mr. Coupland & 3 guests Mr. Fyff/e [second letter "f" crossed with a line] of Merton Mr. Morrs & Mr. Shears.

Monsignor Knox writes his Sherlock Holmes paper in 1910.[134] He read "Studies in Sherlock Holmes" to the Gryphon Club of Trinity College, Oxford on 13 March 1911.[135] Knox's essay was the impetus for "Higher Criticism" of the Canon.

When reading some of these entries of the minutes they take the form of notations perhaps written after the meeting had ended rather than when the meeting was in session. The writings are short, with some having abbreviations, strikethroughs, pencil insertions, and scribbles that seem to suggest this type of record.

Reverend Knox takes part in a reading

The 541st meeting recorded in the *Gryphon Book* has the Reverend Ronald A. Knox taking a part in a translation of the *Troades* by Professor Gilbert Murray. *Troades* (The Trojan Women) is a tragedy written by the Roman playwright Seneca the Younger around 54 CE. Seneca's play, explores the consequences of war for both the victors and the defeated.

The 541st meeting of the Society was held in Mr. Macgregor's rooms on Monday, February 26th, at 8 pm.

---

[134] Reported in *Spiritual Aeneid*, p. 121.
[135] Published in Oxford *Blue Book* of 1912.

In public business, Prof Gilbert Murray's Translation of the Troades was read. The Professor took the largest part, others being distributed amongst Rev. R. Knox, Messrs. Tiddy, Copland, Graeme Paterson, etc. The reading was followed by a short discussion., & the Society adjourned at 10:30 pm.

There were present as visitors:

Mr. Graeme Paterson, late of the Society

Mr. E.N. Marshall

Mr. Pedley

Mr. Rodley (Balliol)

Mr. Ogilvie (Balliol)

R.H. Shears

hon, Sec.

Gilbert Murray was the Regius Professor of Greek and a distinguished classical scholar at the University of Oxford from 1908-1936. Henry VIII founded the chair by 1541 when the first Regis Chair was appointed. Murray is best known as a translator of Greek drama. He translated Euripides for the Oxford Classical Text series; his text appeared in three volumes in 1902, 1904 and 1909. He refused a knighthood in 1912.

Professor Murray disapproved the translation and elucidation of a set of texts that was a common practice for undergraduates. Few Oxford dons edited texts; Murray was not only one but his scholarship rose above the others. His literary approach to studying Greek and Greece and the editing of these texts against strict textual scholarship set him apart from most of the others teaching at the university. The common practice was to teach students to translate from and into Greek.

This conventional procedure is described when Mr. Hilton Soames, tutor and lecturer at the College of St. Luke's, engages Sherlock Holmes to find the student who has copied the examination paper of a Greek translation:

"I must explain to you, Mr. Holmes, that to-morrow is the first day of the

examination for the Fortescue Scholarship. I am one of the examiners.

My subject is Greek, and the first of the papers consists of a large passage of Greek translation which the candidate has not seen."

(The Adventure of the Three Students)

He translated plays into edited texts for teaching purposes rather than to be judged by other professional scholars. This he did with Euripides work. His translations of Greek drama were intended to be acted on stage rather than for student exercises to translate them from a text. He believed that translation went beyond literal meaning. An example was his translation of *Trojan Women*, which was better theatre, but also received criticism for this version that deviated from the conventional. One critic was T.S. Eliot who disliked the poetic models used by Murray.[136] Murray read his translations to his students who enjoyed them more than they did the Greek coursework that they felt was not as interesting. His peers valued his literary approach of Greek and Greece against the scholarship of strict literal translations that were required course mandates.

It was within this forum that the reading of the *Troades* took place in Macgregor's room with Professor Murray taking the largest part and the students participating in round robin readings that included Father Knox.

Father Knox reads "Ella Wheeler Whilcox [sic] Wilcox"

Another entry, 574th, revealed another reading by Monsignor Knox of a paper by Ella Wheeler Whilcox [sic] Wilcox:

---

[136] See Francis West, *Gilbert Murray: A Life* (Beckenham Kent: Croom Helm, Ltd. 1984), of his biography.

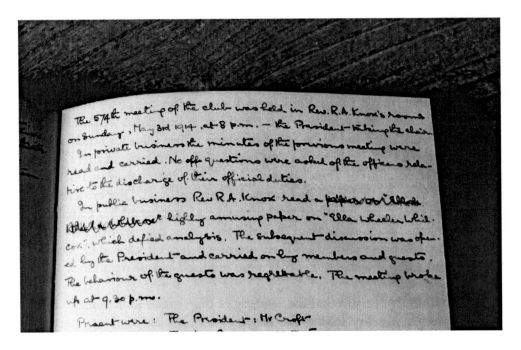

The 574th meeting of the club was held in Rev. R.A. Knox's rooms
on Sunday, May 3rd 1914, at 8 p.m. – The President taking the chair.

In private business the minutes of the previous meeting were read
and carried. No questions were asked of the officers relative to the
discharge of their official duties.

In public business Rev R.A. Knox read a [scribble through of words]
highly amusing paper on "Ella Wheeler Whilcox", which defied analysis.
The subsequent discussion was open. The behaviour of the guests was
regrettable. The meeting broke up at 9:30 p.m.

Ella Wheeler Wilcox (1850-1919) was an American poet who published in many
magazines, periodicals, and books. One wonders what caused the guests to behave in a
"regrettable" manner. A popular poem she wrote was, "Solitude," in 1883 that was
published in the *New York Sun*. It is difficult to believe this was the poem read with the
words, although memorable, "Laugh, and the world laughs with you; Weep, and you
weep alone," might have caused a raucous. However, among her many writings a
possible contender could have been *Drops of Water*, published in 1872 by the National
Temperance Society and Publication House, New York. This book consisted of a
collection of poems many dealing against indulgences with beer, wine, and alcohol.

Some of the titles are, A Glass of Wine," "Alcohol's Requiem upon Prof. P.F.K.," "A Tumbler of Claret," "Don't Drink," "Origin of the Liquor Dealer," and "PH. Best & Co.'s Lager-Beer."

Ella Wheeler Wilcox had long been interested in spiritualism. After the death of her husband in 1916 she wrote a series of columns and made attempts to contact her husband's spirit. Curious? Who else comes to mind?

Holywell Press Limited

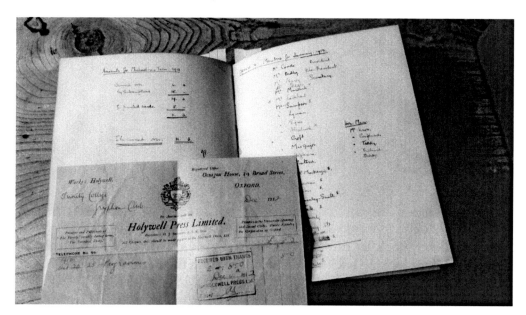

The Gryphon Book has accounting notations with receipts inserted within some of the pages. This particular entry contains the receipt from Holywell Press Limited for 25 programmes.

Trinity College – The Campus

Time spent in the library was a special privilege. Surrounded by the many books that contain so much knowledge to be learned over an extended period of history was an inspiring experience. The works I read and reviewed provided a first-hand account of the events that took place among the members and visitors that attended the Gryphon Club meetings in 1911. Monsignor Knox's papers and the *Gryphon Book of Minutes* served as primary sources of these historical events.

We began a tour of the beautifully manicured campus with Sharon as our guide. We were impressed with the picturesque buildings and landscape of the college. The photo below is the lawns leading out to the Parks Road gates and onto Parks Road. The photo is specifically of the border on the right side of the lawns (as seen when looking towards college) abutting St John's college (which is the other side of the wall).

The walkway took us directly into the Garden Quad. This second photograph also shows the lawns looking back towards college from the Parks Road gates.

This photo also shows the lawns looking back towards college from the Parks Road gates. Garden quad is directly in front of you. The garden buildings are primarily college accommodation and Knox apparently stayed in a room on the left of the Quad. This would be behind the building which is the foreground on the left of the picture - which is the end of a building from Durham Quad.

The photo below is a closer image of the right side of Garden Quad. Father Knox's room was located in the corner of the Garden Quad to the right of the right-hand of the door.

Nicholas Utechin writes that Ronald Knox's room No. 84 was located on the ground floor.

The Dining Hall

The Chapel

The chapel (dating to 1694) and the Hall built in the 18th century would have been here long before Father Knox. We can likely assume that Father Knox spent much of his time in the Dining Hall, and a good many hours in the Chapel.

As we walked through the gates we bid farewell to Susan and departing by the door we found ourselves on Broad Street bustling with people along this main street and the branches of the side streets.

Merton College – Father Ronald A. Knox's First Reading

However, this visit prompted another to Merton College where it has been determined that this may have been the first reading by Father Knox of his paper to the members of the Bodley Club.

Merton College (Father Knox gave first reading)

I visited Merton College and spoke with Julian Reid, archivist. He told me that Ronald Knox read his paper, "The Mind and Art of Sherlock Holmes" to Merton's Bodley Club on Friday 10th March 1911, in the room of Reginald Diggle, one student member of the club. He further stated that the room where the paper was delivered has not yet been established. However, the minutes of the meeting were reproduced earlier this year in an article by Nicholas Utechin.[137]

This first reading of the paper, "The Mind and Art of Sherlock Holmes," three days before Father Knox read it again in his rooms, "Studies in Sherlock Holmes," and then later published as "Studies in the Literature of Sherlock Holmes," with some revisions has sparked controversy. The question is, "Who is the originator of the "Sherlockian critique."

At this point, I digress from continuity of the Oxford visit to comment on the debate that has initiated some controversy.

Knox's Influence

Upon returning home to the United States, I reread two publications of Nicholas Utechin and one written by Michael J. Crowe's. I also read the dialogue between Dr. Sveum and Mr. Lellenberg, "Disputation, Confrontations, and Dialectical Hullabaloo." Mr. Lellenberg argues that it was not Father Knox who was the originator of the

---

[137] See Nicholas Utechin, "The Case of the First Reading." *The Baker Street Journal*, vol. 61. no. 1 (Spring, 2011): 34-47.

"Sherlockian critique" but Frank Sidgwich, in *The Cambridge Review* and Arthur Bartlett Maurice in *The Bookman* who preceded Monsignor Knox in their critical review of Sherlock Holmes.[138] Mr. Lellenberg states that Mr. Maurice continued for 25 years, and that Edgar Smith cited these two gentlemen in his *The Incunabular Sherlock Holmes* and not Father Knox. And although Mr. Lellenberg does not credit either Mr. Sidgwick or Mr. Maurice, or Mr. Knox, or Mr. Lang (a person who also wrote a critical analysis), he does credit S. C. Roberts as the founder of critical analysis who permeated the thoughts of the Baker Street Irregulars and the Sherlock Holmes Society in 1934.

Michael J. Crowe writes that Ronald Knox and his three brothers sent Arthur Conan Doyle a letter that stated inconsistencies in the stories that were published during this period. The letter was dated 1904 or thereabouts, and signed "Sign of Four" to designate the four Knox brothers.[139] The letter may have served as the back drop for Knox's book *Juxta Salices* (By the Side of the Willow) in his "A Decalogue Symposium." The copy of the reply letter by Conan Doyle was first received by Michael J. Crowe from the Earl of Oxford and Asquith, Knox's literacy executor by way of Mrs. Penelope Fitzgerald, Evoe Knox's daughter.[140] Edgar W. Smith writes that five persons from 1902 to 1905 also delved into the inconsistencies of the stories.[141] Crowe states, "If all the relevant writings of these five authors were combined, it would make an essay only slightly larger than Knox's "Studies." He feels credit for Sherlockian scholarship belongs to Knox. As did S.C. Roberts acknowledge Father Knox's influence when he wrote, "For it was Monsignor Knox's famous essay that first beckoned me to Baker Street."[142] Likewise, Jody Baker proclaimed Christopher Morley as the propagator of Holmesianship after Knox. He writes that it was Knox's work advocated by Morley that made the work a seminal piece in Sherlockian scholarship.[143]

I agree with Mr. John Lisenmeyer, and Mr. Dmitri Jarintzoff that Ronald A. Knox was focused on finding the inconsistencies of the Sherlock Holmes stories in a *humorous*

---

[138] "Disputation, Confrontation, and dialectical Hullabaloo," http://www.bsiarchivalhistory.org/BSI_Archival_History/Disputations_dept.html. See also, Jon Lellenberg, "The Ronald Knox Myth." *The Sherlock Holmes Journal*, vol. 30, no. 2 (Summer 2011), 53-58.

[139] Crowe, pp. 6-7.

[140] Ibid, p. 13-14.

[141] Edgar W. Smith, *The Incunabular Sherlock Holmes* (Morristown, N.J.: Baker Street Irregulars, 1958).

[142] See Preface, S.C. Roberts, *Holmes & Watson: A Miscellany*, (New York: Otto Penzler Books). Reprinted by arrangement with Oxford University Press, 1953.

[143] Jody Baker, "In the Beginning was Ronald Knox." Retrieved August 20, 2011, http://members.cox.net/sherlock1/grand.htm

rather than undertaking a serious examination as he had done with biblical writings that he felt demanded a "Higher Order" of scholarship.[144] Within the same entry of the Merton College's Bodley Club minutes, entry 203rd meeting, of 10 March 1911, was a statement by Mr. Hutton, an ex-president of the Bodley Club who stated that, "Mr. Knox's paper was certainly the most brilliant paper the Bodley Club had ever heard, and he considered that it would pave the way for making the study of Sherlock Holmes a University subject."[145] It is clear that Father Knox's paper influenced the members of the Bodley Club just as it did when read to the members of the Gryphon Club.

Knox's influence on the art of Sherlockian scholarship is further attested by Christopher Morley who recognized his writing of "Studies in the Literature of Sherlock Holmes" in the humorous way in which it was intended:

> The device of pretending to analyze matters of amusement with full severity is
>
> the best way to reproach those who approach the highest subjects with too literal
>
> a mind. This new frolic in criticism was welcome at once; those who were students
>
> at Oxford in that ancient day remember how Mr. Knox was invited round from
>
> college to college to reread his agreeable lampoon; it was first printed in a journal
>
> of undergruate highbrows (*The Blue Book*) then appropriately edited by W. H. I.
>
> Watson.[146]

Closing

Of course, there were sightseeing walks and a visit to the local sites such as the White Horse and the Eagle and Child, known locally as Bird and Child, frequented by J.R.R. Tolkien and his friend C.J. Lewis who had a pint or two and smoked their pipes in their day. More recently Inspector Morse and Inspector Lewis included these two sites among the many in Oxford in their filming for the Masterpiece Mystery television series. We enjoyed a meal during our two day stay at these two establishments, and also managed a stop at the Randolph Hotel which Colin Dexter included in his Inspector

---

[144] See John Lisenmeyer, "Knox and After: 1911-2011, A Century of Scholarship." *Baker Street Journal*, vol. 61. No. 1 (Spring , 2011): 25-33.; also, Nicholas Utechin, "The Case of the First Reading," *Baker Street Journal*, vol. 61. No. 1 (Spring, 2011): 34-47, recorded minutes of the Bodley Club where Dmitri. Jarintzoff , secretary, comments are stated.

[145] Utechin, 2011, p. 37.

[146] Steven Rothman, *The Standard Doyle Company: Christopher Morley on Sherlock Holmes*. (New York: Fordham University Press, 1990), 7.

Morse stories. I was told by Sharon that Colin Dexter was a frequent visitor to Trinity College and that scenes for the Inspector Lewis series were continuing to be shot at the college's location.

On our earlier visit to Oxford I had purchased a copy of Dorothy L. Sayers *Unpopular Opinions* and *Studies in Sherlock Holmes: I. Oxford or Cambridge* by O. F. Grazebrook at Blackwell's Bookshop. On this visit I was able to make some purchases one of which was a book written by Charles Higham on the life of Conan Doyle which is very interesting and informative.[147]

The experience of visiting Trinity College, meeting Sharon Cure, reading the papers and historical text she made available and the time she extended to my wife and me as we toured the campus are memorable.

---

[147] Charles Higham, *The Adventures of Conan Doyle: The Life of the Creator of Sherlock Holmes* (London: Hamish Hamilton, 1976).

PART 3

Magic Squares
and a
Cinquain

Magic Squares

Magic Squares have been used by elementary, high school, and postsecondary levels throughout many years. Teachers have used Magic Squares by developing them to include course content and statements or examples that enable students to review their understanding of the key concepts and facts being studied. Christopher Morley developed a Magic Square which he called "The Mycroft Magic Square."[148] Another, form is the crossword puzzle that appeared in the *Baker Street Journal*[149] as did other types of puzzles in other issues. One of the issues reprinted a crossword puzzle from the *Manchester Guardian Weekly*.[150] Of most interest was the posting that appeared giving credit to John J. Mc Aleer who sent it to the *Boston Globe* about Rev. Ronald A. Knox.

> One morning on his way from London to Oxford by train, he sat down
>
> next to an elderly lady. Opening his copy of the London *Times* to the
>
> crossword puzzle, he sat for a few minutes staring at it. His companion,
>
> perhaps aware that the *Times* puzzle is reputedly the world's most difficult,
>
> asked, "Would you like a pencil?" "No, thanks," replied Knox. "Just finished."

Crossword puzzles, SUDOKO, Scrambled Words, and others, in kind, may present a complexity that needs to be understood before being solved. However, once we do, the other side of this complexity is simplicity when knowing the puzzle's secret. Reading a mystery is like solving a puzzle. It presents us with complexities that we try to untangle as we read and think about the clues. However, once the mystery is solved, more than likely, it simplifies the complexity and makes the resolution more meaningful.

When I was invested in the Nashville Scholars of The Three Pipe Problem, I chose the name Professor Coram and developed this magic square to commemorate this distinctive honor. The closing numbers that spell **LEAGUE** reifies the theme and pays tribute to the membership that comprises The Nashville Scholars of the Three Pipe Problem.

---

[148] See "The Mycroft Magic Square," in Steven Rothman, *The Standard Doyle Company: Christopher Morley on Sherlock Holmes.* (New York: Fordham University Press, 1990), 232-234.

[149] Donald A. Yates, "An Unsolved Baskerville Puzzle," *Baker Street Journal*, vol.7, no. 2 (April, 1957): 84-87.

[150] An early publication of the *Baker Street Journal*, vol. 2, no. 2, 1947, 208-209, showed a crossword puzzle developed by Stephen Saxe; another, "Sherlockian Crossword," *Baker Street Journal*, vol. 16, no. 1 (March, 1966): 50-51;. also, F.V. Morley, "A Sherlock Holmes Cross-Word." In Vincent Starrett., *221B Studies in Sherlock Holmes*, (New York: Macmillan 1940).

The major theme of this magic square is revealed on the diagonal line from upper left to lower right. I began by first writing on the top and left side – **THE SCHOLARS** – as a referent to our scion: Nashville Scholars of the Three Pipe Problem. Then I wrote diagonally - **3 PIPE PROBE** - as a variation of the credo of our organization's affiliated adventure The Red-Headed League. Then as a corresponding tie to the theme I wrote vertically on the last column **S BRIAR PIPE** to signify the use of Sherlock's Briar Pipe during his contemplation's of the adventures. In spaces 89 and 90, I inserted the initials **B and P** as a clue to this vertical message. If you wish to complete this Magic Square, follow and complete the instructions.

Begin by filling in the numbers that correspond with the statement or title of the adventure using capital letters. The numbers given after each statement or adventure designates a completion of that item. Continue filling in the consecutive numbers along the continuum from left to right proceeding downward until all spaces have been filled. It is not necessary to answer the statements or titles in the order in which they appear.

NASHVILLE SCHOLARS OF THE 3 PIPE PROBLEM

	T	H	E	S	C	H	O	L	A	R	S
H	1	2	3	4	5	6	7	8	9	10	
E	11	12	13	14	15	16	17	18	19	20	
S	21	22	23	24	25	26	27	28	29	30	
C	31	32	33	34	35	36	37	38	39	40	
H	41	42	43	44	45	46	47	48	49	50	
O	51	52	53	54	55	56	57	58	59	60	
L	61	62	63	64	65	66	67	68	69	70	
A	71	72	73	74	75	76	77	78	79	80	
R	81	82	83	84	85	86	87	88	89	90	
S	91	92	93	94	95	96	97	98	99	100	

Numeric three and name of adventure.
1, 2, 3, 4, 5, 6, 7, 8, 9, 10
Initials of the Illustrator of SH adventures.
11, 12
*The Missing Three-*_____
13, 14, 15, 16, 17, 18, 19
SH trained in Japanese self-defense named _____
20, 21, 22, 23, 24, 25, 26
The Sign of the _____
27, 28, 29 30
The Adventure of the _____ *Napoleons.*
31, 32, 33
The Adventure of the Bruce-Partington _____
34, 35, 36, 37, 38
The Adventure of the Golden _____ - _____
39, 40, 41, 42, 43, 44, 45, 46
Professor _____
47, 48, 49, 50, 51
The Problem of _____ *Bridge.*
52, 53, 54, 55
The Five Orange Pips minus four.
56, 57, 58
SH's faithful companion.
59, 60, 61, 62, 63, 64, 65, 66
The Adventure of the _____ *Circle.*
67, 68, 69
The Final _____
70, 71, 72, 73, 74, 75, 76
The _____ *Cyclist.*
77, 78, 79, 80, 81, 82, 83, 84
The Adventure of the _____ *Carbuncle.*
85, 86, 87, 88
First letter of "Briar" and also of "Pipe."
89, 90
The Adventure of the Lion's _____ .
91, 92, 93, 94
The Red-Headed _____ .
95, 96, 97, 98, 99, 100

Clues

1. Diagonal reveals the *Cryptograph* theme – 1, 12, 23, 34, 45, 56, 67, 78, 89, 100
2. Use 89 and 90 to solve 10, 20, 30, 40, 50, 60, 70, 80, 90, 100
3. Closing related to theme: 95, 96, 97, 98, 99, 100

THE SCHOLARS: *Magic Squares*

ANSWERS and CLUES

1 – 10 = 3 GARRIDEBS
11 – 12 = BP
13 – 19 = QUARTER
20 – 26 = BARITSU
27 – 30 = FOUR
31 – 33 = SIX
34 – 38 = PLANS
39 – 46 = PINCE NEZ
47 – 51 = CORAM
52 – 55 = THOR
56 – 58 = PIP
59 – 66 = DR WATSON
67 – 69 = RED
70 – 76 = PROBLEM
77 – 84 = SOLITARY
85 – 88 = BLUE
89 – 90 = BP
91 – 94 = MANE
95 – 100 = LEAGUE

Clues

1. Diagonal reveals the *Cryptograph* theme – 1, 12, 23, 34, 45, 56, 67, 78, 89, 100

- **3 PIPE PROBE**

2. Use 89 and 90 to solve 10, 20, 30, 40, 50, 60, 70, 80, 90, 100

- **BP**
- **S BRIAR PIPE** (Sherlock's Briar Pipe)

3. Closing related to theme: 95, 96, 97, 98, 99, 100

- **LEAGUE** (*The Adventure of the Red-Headed League*)

CINQUAIN

A Cinquain is a poem and can result in a perfect paragraph. It has a variety of uses and can be used in any subject. The form of a Cinquain has five lines.

Directions

5 Lines
- 1st Line - Name of something (Noun)
- 2nd Line - Two adjectives which describe the noun in line 1.
- 3rd Line - Three action verbs ending in *ing*.
- 4th Line - Four word phrase which captures the essence of what you are describing.
- 5th Line - One word noun may be the same or synonymous with the word on line 1.

_____

_____   _____

_____   _____   _____

_____   _____   _____   _____

_____

An example:

Scholars

Energetic   Deliberate

Reading   Contemplating   Discussing

Studying the Sherlockian stories

Nashville

An alternate four word phrase could be:

                              Scholars
                  Energetic   Deliberate

Reading   Contemplating   Discussing

                Studying a three pipe problem

                          Nashville

A paragraph is then developed which reads:

Our scholars are energetic and deliberate in their readings,
contemplations, and discussions of the Sherlockian stories.
Each story requires careful study and may take as much
time as it would to smoke three pipefuls of tobacco. The
Nashville Scholars of the Three Pipe Problem is a scion
worthy of its name.

There are many ways to use the Cinquain in scions or in schools. A starter could
be a character in a story or a title of a story.

Example:
                          (Character)
                              or
      (Title of the Story (e.g., The Adventure of the Speckled Band)

                    _____   _____

          _____   _____   _____

    _____   _____   _____   _____

              _____

EPILOGUE

The essays that appear in this volume, like others appearing in the *Baker Street Journal*, *Sherlock Holmes Journal*, or Sherlockian books devoted to the art of essays, are somewhat unique in that mixed genres are used in taking narrative stories and infusing them with factual information. This task demands knowledge of the events taking place in the story and then focusing on those aspects that can be related to a factual person, place, setting, or object within a historical, political, cultural, scientific, or societal context. Putting oneself into the Victorian era and then thinking retrospectively about the conditions and events that prompted these stories is an important role of the reader.

"The Stock-Broker's Clerk: Parallels and Parodies" and "Thumb-less in Eyford" are examples of essays that require the reader to extract those incidents that are contrary to realistic events as depicted in the stories. They are intended to be humorous renditions that are studied and then extracted through plausible interpretations from implausible contexts. Other essays are guided by opinions and use of plausible facts that can be argued as relevant to fictional contexts and circumstances that go beyond the readings such as "Sherlock Holmes As College Professor."

"2 +2 ≠ 4?" addresses Monsignor Ronald A. Knox's admonition to Watson, "You know my methods, Watson: apply them! This essay required reading Knox's "Studies in the Literature of Sherlock Holmes" and then using the information gleaned from the writing to inquire whether or not Watson knew Sherlock Holmes' methods, and if so, why he couldn't apply them. In a real sense, each of us is a Watson when reading the Sherlock Holmes stories. Reading the stories provides instances of Sherlock Holmes' reasoning and the bewilderment of Watson trying and failing to answer the question.

An article written in 1946, in the first volume of the *Baker Street Journal*, asks why there are three missing words in the American edition of *The Valley of Fear*? My review of the literature indicated that this question had yet to be addressed or resolved. By reviewing the conditions that existed in the mining communities in Pennsylvania and the role of the Molly McGuires and the Coal and Iron Police, a supposition was formed, researched, and then put into words, "The Valley of Fear: Three Missing Words."

Wanting an opportunity to visit the falls where Sherlock Holmes met his demise, I visited the Reichenbach Falls to view the landscape. A trip to nearby Trummelbach Falls provided a comparison of waterfalls that led to writing, "Footprints Along the Paths: Reichenbach Falls and Trummelbach Falls." The force of the Trummelbach waterfalls and the roar echoing through the caverns would also have been a fitting setting for the struggle between Sherlock Holmes and Professor Moriarty. "Trinity College Oxford and the Gryphon Book" includes photographs of the college and transcriptions of the minutes written in the Gryphon Book. This trip offered a unique opportunity to again visit Oxford and view the papers of Reverend Ronald A. Knox and the entries recorded in the *Gryphon Book of Minutes*. The educational value of this experience will always be most memorable. This travelogue to both sites and to Oxford offered a first-hand experience with the places, settings and the artifacts that continue to lure me to Sherlock Holmes and his adventures.

I couldn't resist an urge to write a short narrative placing Sherlock Holmes and Dr. Watson in Schenectady, New York. I spent a good part of my life in Schenectady and also coached football at Bishop Gibbons High School and Union College. The city has been named in many films, television shows, and commercials throughout the years due, in part, to its historical significance in colonial times, and its unusual pronunciation. The lecture tour arranged by Major Pond during A. Conan Doyle's visit to the United States provided the backdrop for this writing, "Sherlock Holmes, American Football, and Schenectady."

The appendices within some of the essays contain the use of a thematic organizer to activate the reader's knowledge of a target concept before reading. The steps for developing a thematic organizer are provided so that a parent, guardian, or teacher can develop one for a learner to use before reading a text; an example is shown. Also, a visual literacy guide is shown after the essay, "Sherlock Holmes Revealed in Art." This type of guide is easy to develop and has been found to be an effective adjunct aid for learners to use when viewing a visual such as a painting, graph, chart, table, illustration, cartoon, figure, musical notes as in an arrangement, mathematical formula, and so forth. It aids learners in noticing the features of material and also by reacting to the interpretive statements that require further examination of the visual display. Likewise, the use of Magic Squares and Cinquains actively engage users in the process of solving puzzles and creating a new work.

The stories of Sherlock Holmes represent events occurring in the Victoria time period. They have captured the interest of readers spanning over a hundred years. The events portrayed in the stories have been analyzed, dissected, criticized, praised, copied, and expanded in a variety of nuances from drawings, paintings, cartoons, serious scholarship, humorous renditions, comic books, magazine articles, graphic novels, pastiches, books, films, and television revisions. Ideas from these events of the past continue (to the amazement of some) to be written about Sherlock Holmes. Evidence the writings that continue to appear in respected journals such as the *Baker Street Journal*, the *Sherlock Holmes Journal*, and stories appearing in *The Strand Magazine*.

For those not yet acquainted with Conan Doyle's world of Sherlock Holmes, a journey that brings forth a new experience that goes well beyond a story's ending awaits. The stories will involve you in the Victorian writing style of the period, give you a pleasurable pastime, and stir your imagination to realize unforeseen possibilities. Once a story is read, a reflective examination may prompt a path toward further readings of the events that take you into a new world of imagination and enterprise. Perhaps these essays will help you enter that new world of imagination beyond the original stories.

About the Author

Marino Carlos Alvarez is professor emeritus in the Department of Teaching and Learning of the College of Education and a senior researcher and Director of the Exploring Minds Project in the Center of Excellence in Information Systems at Tennessee State University. He received his associate in arts degree from the Junior College of Albany and his bachelor's degree from Fort Lewis College. His master's and doctoral degrees are from West Virginia University. He has taught social studies at the junior and high school levels. He has served on international and national committees, editorial advisory boards, and was a Past President of the Association of Literacy Educators and Researchers and Past Chair of the Action Research Special Interest Group of the American Educational Research Association. Dr. Alvarez is the recipient of the Laureate Award given for life-time achievement in research, publications, and teaching by the Association of Literacy Educators and Researchers, and is a co-author with Bob Gowin of *The Art of Educating with V Diagrams* published by Cambridge University Press, and *The Little Book: Conceptual Elements of Research* published by Rowman & Littlefield. Professor Alvarez is a Sherlockian and an invested member of the Nashville Scholars of the Three Pipe Problem, the Fresh Rashers of Nashville, and a member of the Beacon Society, and the Sherlock Holmes Society of London. He has published in the *Baker Street Journal*. Dr. Alvarez is the first faculty member to be granted professor emeritus status and the only recipient of both the *Teacher-of-the-Year* and the *Distinguished Researcher-of-the-Year* Awards at Tennessee State University.

Suggested Readings

Baring-Gould, William S. *The Aannotated Sherlock Holmes*, vols. 1 & 2. New York: Clarkson N. Potter, Inc., Publisher, 1967.

Baring-Gould, William S. *Sherlock Holmes of Baker Street*. New York: Clarkson N. Potter, 1962.

Clarkson, Stephen. *The Canonical Compendium*. Ashcroft, British Columbia: Calabash Press, 1999.

Crowe, Michael J. *Ronald Knox and Sherlock Holmes*. Indianapolis: Gasogene Books, 2011.

Dahlinger. S.E., and Klinger, Leslie S. *Sherlock Holmes, Conan Doyle & The Bookman*. Indianapolis: Gasogene Books, 2010.

Dakin, D. Martin. *A Sherlock Holmes Commentary*. New York: Drake Publishers, 1972.

Doyle, Arthur Conan. *Memories & Adventures*. Oxford: Oxford University Press, 1989.

Doyle, Arthur Conan. *The Adventures of Sherlock Holmes. Vols. 1, II*. New York: Heritage Press, 1950. A definitive text, corrected and edited by Edgar W. Smith, with an introduction by Vincent Starrett, and illustrations by Frederic Dore Steele, Sidney Paget and others.

Doyle, Arthur Conan. *The Complete Sherlock Holmes*. Garden City, New York: Doubleday & Company, 1905.

Doyle, P.J. and McDiarmid, E.W. *The Baker Street Dozen*. New York: Congdon & Weed, 1987.

Duncan, Alistair. *Eliminate the Impossible: An Examination of the World of Sherlock Holmes on Page and Screen*. Stanstead Abbotts, Hertfordshire: MX Publishing, 2008.

Edwards, Owen Dudley. *The Quest for Sherlock Holmes*. Harmondsworth, Middlesex, England: Penguin Books Ltd, .1984.

Gerber, Samuel M. *Chemistry and Crime: From Sherlock Holmes to Today's Courtroom*. Washington, D.C.: American Chemical Society, 1983.

Gerber, Samuel M. and Saferstein, Richard. *More Chemistry and Crime: From Marsh Arsenic Test to DNA Profile*. Washington, D.C.: American Chemical Society, 1997.

Green, Joseph and Watt, Peter Ridgway. *Alas, Poor Sherlock*. Kent, England: Chancery House Press, 2007.

Higham, Charles. *The Adventures of Conan Doyle: The Life of the Creator of Sherlock Holmes*. London: Hamish Hamilton, 1976.

Hines, Stephen and Womack, Steven. *The True Crime Files of Sir Arthur Conan Doyle*. New York: Berkley Prime Crime, 2001.

Holroyd, James Edward. *Seventeen Steps to 221B*. London: George Allen & Unwin, 1967.

Kaye, Marvin. *The Game is Afoot*. New York: St. Martin's Press, 1994.

Keating, H.R.F. *Sherlock Holmes: The Man and His World*. New Jersey: Castle Books, 2006.

King, Laurie R. and Klinger, Leslie S. *The Grand Game. Vol. 1. 1902-1959*. New York: The Baker Street Irregulars, 2011.

King, Laurie R. and Klinger, Leslie S. *The Grand Game. Vol. 2. 1960-2009*. New York: The Baker Street Irregulars, 2012.

Klinger, Leslie S. *The New Annotated Sherlock Holmes. Vols. I, II, III*. New York: W. W. Norton & Company, 2005.

Pearsall, Ronald. *Conan Doyle: A Biographical Solution*. Glasgow: Richard Drew Publishing, 1977.

Press, Charles. *Looking Over Sir Arthur's Shoulder*. Shelburne, Ontario: George A. Vadnerburgh, Publisher, 2004.

Redmond, Christopher. *Sherlock Holmes Handbook*, 2 ed. Toronto: Dundurn Press, 2009.

Rennison, Nick. *Sherlock Holmes*. London: Atlantic Books, 2005.

Roberts, S.C. *Holmes & Watson*. New York: Otto Penzler Books. Reprinted by arrangement with Oxford University Press, 1953.

Rothman, Steven. *The Standard Doyle Company: Christopher Morley on Sherlock Holmes*. New York: Fordham University Press, 1990.

Sauvage, Leo. *Sherlockian Heresies*. Edited with an Introduction by Julie McKuras and Susan Vizoskie. Indianapolis: Gasogene Books, 2010.

Shreffler, Philip A. *Sherlock Holmes by Gas-Lamp*. New York: Fordham University Press, 1989.

Starrett, Vincent. *The Private Life of Sherlock Holmes*. Chicago: The University of Chicago Press, 1960.

Stashower, Daniel. *Teller of Tales*. New York: Henry Holf and Company, 1999.

Tracy, Jack. *The Encyclopaedia Sherlockiana*. New York: Avenel, 1987.

Van Liere, Edward J. *A Doctor Enjoys Sherlock Holmes*. New York: Vantage Press, 1959.

Wagner, E.J. *The Science of Sherlock Holmes*. New Jersey: John Wiley & Sons, 2006.

Also from MX Publishing

Close To Holmes

A Look at the Connections Between
Historical London, Sherlock
Holmes and Sir Arthur Conan
Doyle.

Eliminate The Impossible

An Examination of the World of
Sherlock Holmes on Page and
Screen.

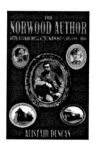

The Norwood Author

Arthur Conan Doyle and the
Norwood Years (1891 - 1894) –
Winner of the 2011 Howlett Literary
Award (Sherlock Holmes book of the
year)

www.mxpublishing.com

Also From MX Publishing

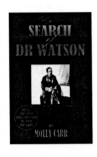

In Search of Dr Watson

Wonderful biography of
Dr.Watson from expert Molly
Carr – 2nd edition fully updated.

Arthur Conan Doyle, Sherlock
Holmes and Devon

A Complete Tour Guide and
Companion.

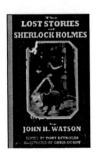

The Lost Stories of Sherlock Holmes

Eight more stories from the pen of John
H Watson – compiled by Tony
Reynolds.

www.mxpublishing.com

Also From MX Publishing

Watsons Afghan Adventure

Fascinating biography of Watson's time in Afghanistan from US Army veteran Kieran McMullen.

Shadowfall

Sherlock Holmes, ancient relics and demons and mystic characters. A supernatural Holmes pastiche.

Official Papers of The Hound of The Baskervilles

Very unusual collection of the original police papers from The Hound case.

www.mxpublishing.com

Also From MX Publishing

The Sign of Fear

The first adventure of the 'female Sherlock Holmes'. A delightful fun adventure with your favourite supporting Holmes characters.

A Study in Crimson

The second adventure of the 'female Sherlock Holmes' with a host of sub-plots and new characters joining Watson and Fanshaw

The Chronology of Arthur Conan Doyle

The definitive chronology used by historians and libraries worldwide.

www.mxpublishing.com

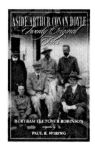
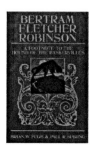

Also From MX Publishing

Bobbles and Plum

Four playlets from PG Wodehouse
'lost' for over 100 years – found
and reprinted with an excellent
commentary

The World of Vanity Fair

A specialist full-colour reproduction
of key articles from Bertram Fletcher
Robinson containing of colour
caricatures from the early 1900s.

Tras Las He huellas de Arthur
Conan Doyle (in Spanish)

Un viaje ilustrado por Devon.

www.mxpublishing.com

The Outstanding Mysteries of
Sherlock Holmes

With thirteen Homes stories and
illustrations Kelly re-creates the
gas-lit, fog-enshrouded world of
Victorian London

Rendezvous at The Populaire

Sherlock Holmes has retired,
injured from an encounter with
Moriarty. He's tempted out of
retirement for an epic battle with
the Phantom of the opera.

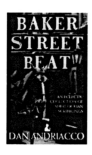

Baker Street Beat

An eclectic collection of articles,
essays, radio plays and 'general
scribblings' about Sherlock Holmes
from Dr.Dan Andriacco.

www.mxpublishing.com

Also From MX Publishing

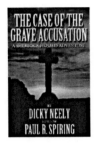

The Case of The Grave Accusation

The creator of Sherlock Holmes has
been accused of murder. Only
Holmes and Watson can stop the
destruction of the Holmes legacy.

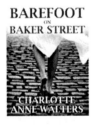

Barefoot on Baker Street

Epic novel of the life of a Victorian
workhouse orphan featuring
Sherlock Holmes and Moriarty.

Case of Witchcraft

A tale of witchcraft in the Northern
Isles, in which long-concealed secrets
are revealed -- including some that
concern the Great Detective himself!

www.mxpublishing.com

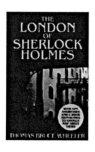

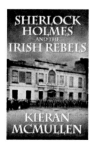
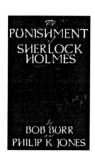
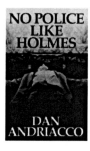

Also From MX Publishing

In The Night, In The Dark

Winner of the Dracula Society Award
– a collection of supernatural ghost
stories from the editor of the Sherlock
Holmes Society of London journal.

Sherlock Holmes and
The Lyme Regis Horror

Fully updated 2nd edition of this
bestselling Holmes story set in Dorset.

My Dear Watson

Winner of the Suntory Mystery Award
for fiction and translated from the
original Japanese. Holmes greatest
secret is revealed – Sherlock Holmes is
a woman.

www.mxpublishing.com

Lightning Source UK Ltd.
Milton Keynes UK
UKOW022020200613

212615UK00001B/1/P